"The Travels of Daniel Ascher *is about the power of stories, particularly the ones we tell about ourselves. Within its svelte form, the novel packs in a love story (several actually), a family story, a war story, a mystery, a travelogue, and even a convincingly imagined children's adventure series. All these strands weave together beautifully in this deftly plotted and deeply moving novel.*"

—GABRIELLE ZEVIN, AUTHOR OF
THE STORIED LIFE OF A. J. FIKRY

WHO IS THE REAL AUTHOR OF *The Black Insignia*? Is it H. R. Sanders, whose name is printed on the cover of every installment of the wildly successful young adult adventure series? Or is it Daniel Roche, the enigmatic world traveler who disappears for months at a time? When Daniel's great-niece, Hélène, moves to Paris to study archeology, she does not expect to be searching for answers to these questions. As rumors circulate, however, that the twenty-fourth volume of the *Black Insignia* series will be the last, Hélène and her friend Guillaume, a devoted fan of her great-uncle's books, set out to discover more about the man whose life eludes her. In so doing, she uncovers an explosive secret dating back to the darkest days of the Nazi occupation.

"Déborah Lévy-Bertherat's slim novel packs a powerful punch. Is Daniel Ascher a respected children's author? A world traveler? Or a man so grief stricken that he has concocted an elaborate literary mystery? His niece sets out to discover the truth, and in doing so, uncovers a dark family secret. This is a book that both adults and older teens will enjoy as they too seek to find the truth about *The Travels of Daniel Ascher*."

—PAMELA KLINGER-HORN, MAGERS & QUINN BOOKSELLERS (MINNEAPOLIS, MN)

"The story — or rather, stories — of *The Travels of Daniel Ascher* are so rich, multilayered, and moving that it is hard to believe it could all be contained in this small book."

—LYNN ROBERTS, SQUARE BOOKS (OXFORD, MS)

"In *The Travels of Daniel Ascher*, objects are physically hidden in other objects, photographs are not what they seem, there are stories within stories, and a scrap of yellowed paper written in Hebrew may hold the key to everything. I read this novel in a day, in my pajamas, without leaving the sofa. I would recommend the same for anyone."

—LYSBETH ABRAMS, EIGHT COUSINS BOOKSTORE (FALMOUTH, MA)

"Great-uncle Daniel wanders the world and brings back exotic souvenirs from foreign lands. He has done this since Hélène was a small child and his life has always been an intriguing, if vaguely frightening, mystery . . . But Daniel is not really her uncle. He was adopted by her family at the end of World War II. He is a war orphan, a Jew, and he harbors a deep and troubling secret."

—CONRAD SILVERBERG, BOSWELL BOOK COMPANY (MILWAUKEE, WI)

The Travels of Daniel Ascher

The Travels of
Daniel Ascher

Déborah Lévy-Bertherat

TRANSLATED FROM THE FRENCH BY
ADRIANA HUNTER

OTHER PRESS
NEW YORK

Copyright © 2013, Editions Payot & Rivages

First published in France as *Les voyages de Daniel Ascher*
by Editions Payot & Rivages, Paris, in 2013

Translation copyright © 2015 by Adriana Hunter
Production editor: Yvonne E. Cárdenas
Text designer: Julie Fry
Case design & illustrations: Andreas Feher
Painting on page 174 by the author, inspired by Chaim Soutine.
This book was set in Fournier and Syntax.

10 9 8 7 6 5 4 3 2

Library of Congress Cataloging-in-Publication Data
Lévy-Bertherat, Déborah.
  [Voyages de Daniel Ascher. English]
  The travels of Daniel Ascher / by Déborah Lévy-Bertherat ;
translated from the French by Adriana Hunter.
  pages cm
  ISBN 978-1-59051-707-9 (alk. paper) — ISBN 978-1-59051-708-6
1. Authors — Fiction. 2. Plagiarism — Fiction. I. Hunter, Adriana. II. Title.
  PQ2672.E9525V6913 2015
  843'.914 — dc23

                                        2014017156

To Jérôme, Émile, Irène, and Georges

"Deep down, Peter, what is it that makes you love adventure?"

"I don't know..."

He looked out to sea, at the gathering clouds. He had spent his life traveling the oceans and continents, and he occasionally had an urge to put away his suitcases.

Icy sea spray whipped his face. He ran his tongue over his lips. There was the answer: the taste of salt...

— H. R. Sanders, *The Call of Gibraltar*

That boy might be happy if he would stay at home, but if he goes abroad he will be the miserablest Wretch that was ever born.

— Daniel Defoe, *Robinson Crusoe*

PART ONE

September—December 1999

1

Adventures in the Gardens

WHEN HÉLÈNE THINKS BACK TO THAT FALL, her first fall in Paris, what she immediately remembers are her walks through the Luxembourg Gardens with her young neighbor. Jonas developed habits as inflexible as rituals. The moment they were through the gate, he would run and hide in the park keepers' empty hut and close the low door, which afforded only a glimpse of the top of his head. He would wait there a few seconds, just long enough for a lion to prowl around the outside, or for Hélène to look for him and pretend to get worried, then he would leap out with a triumphant laugh.

She used to sit on a bench beside the sandbox and watch him dig; every now and then he would come over to give her a coin he had found and that he wanted her to look after for him. Strolling along the walkways, he picked up smooth, glossy horse chestnuts, filling his pockets and then Hélène's. When there were no more chestnuts, he made bouquets of dead leaves for his mother, and they brought the smell of earth and rain from the gardens right into their home.

3

Guillaume often went along with them. Hélène had not known him long, he was a student in her class at the Institute of Archaeology, where she had finally enrolled after three interminable years studying history in Orléans. At the beginning of the semester she'd immediately noticed how tall he was, and she used to sit two or three rows behind him in class, occasionally letting her eyes settle on the nape of his neck and his very low hairline. They probably shouldn't have become friends. Hélène wanted to seem older than twenty years, she swept her hair up in a chignon, and wore high-heeled shoes and scarlet lipstick. Guillaume was two years older than her but was still passionately connected with anything that reminded him of his childhood: when they went to the Luxembourg Gardens, he'd pay for Jonas to have a ride on the carousel just for the pleasure of watching him. The child would wave excitedly, waggling the stick he was holding to scoop a ring off the peg on the way past. The ring, Guillaume would cry, catch the ring. He wished he, too, were four years old, so he could ride on an elephant. He bought crocodile-shaped candy at the refreshment stall, and ate most of it himself. He told Jonas adventure stories about being lost in the jungles of Burma or the forests of the Amazon; he taught him to mimic the sound of a twin-engine plane in free fall, and Jonas tried so hard to get it right, it made him splutter.

It was on one of these walks, halfway through October, that Guillaume first mentioned *The Black Insignia*. They were sitting on park chairs along the pathway beside the orchard, with their feet up on chairs too. Jonas had lined up lots of gold nuggets he had collected and was counting them methodically. Guillaume then remembered all the collections he'd had as a child, the stamps, the bird feathers, the stones with holes through them, the cherry pips, the cartoons, *Tintin*, *Blake and Mortimer*, and other book series, his favorite of which was *The Black Insignia*. He especially loved the first book, it started with a plane crash in which the hero, the only survivor, was seriously injured. Jonas abandoned his counting to listen to the story.

Hélène stood up because her back and buttocks were stiff from sitting on a metal chair for too long. She walked a little way away and noticed one of the gardeners picking apples on the other side of a fence up ahead of her, how amazing, apples in the middle of Paris. She called the boys over, come and look at this, you won't believe it, but they didn't listen. The gardener filled his basket and went on his way; it was the end of the day, Hélène said it was late, they should go home, they'd soon hear the whistle for closing time. Guillaume headed off toward his neighborhood, promising the child he would carry on with the story next time. Hélène helped Jonas put his pebbles in his pocket and took his hand for the walk home.

2

Under the Eaves

SHE HAD JUST MOVED INTO A LITTLE BEDROOM under the eaves of a building on rue Vavin, very close to the Institute of Archaeology on rue Michelet. Her father's uncle had loaned it to her; he lived on the ground floor, but she hadn't seen him since she arrived, he was away traveling. She didn't have much in common with him, so his absence rather suited her. Her room had a low ceiling and was so narrow that the bed filled its entire width at one end, but it did have a proper window that you could open by kneeling on the bed. From there you could look down into the building's inner courtyard where there was a small tree with a pockmarked trunk and a crack on the wall the shape of an old man's profile; and looking up over the zinc roofs of Paris, you could see the tip of the Eiffel Tower.

She knew Paris a little, but not this neighborhood, between the Montparnasse metro station and the Luxembourg Gardens, and when she first arrived in late September she did a lot of walking around, making the most of the fine weather. In fact that whole fall turned out to be very mild, people should have been wary, but who could have guessed that such violent storms were brewing? Hélène explored the area, looking in shop windows on rue Vavin and rue Bréa: secondhand books, Chinese delis, the woman from the candy store waving hello to the man from the hardware store who was hanging multicolored pails under his awning. In among the dusty bushes on rue Notre-Dame-des-Champs, the rough-hewn statue of Captain Dreyfus hid its face behind a broken saber. Her wanderings gradually took her farther and farther afield.

The neighbors thought she was Mr. Roche's niece, his great-niece, she corrected them, oh, I'm sorry, he seems so young. He hadn't told his family where he was, but his neighbors knew he'd gone to Tierra del Fuego and would be back on October 24, so brave, such a remarkable man, they seemed to her to be talking about a different person. In the early days, one of the neighbors had asked Hélène if she could pick up her son from nursery school, and she had gotten into the habit of taking Jonas to the Luxembourg Gardens twice a week.

ONE AFTERNOON TOWARD THE MIDDLE OF OCTOBER, she met a very old couple by the mailboxes in the entrance to her building. The man raised his Prince of Wales checked hat, revealing an archipelago of age spots on his balding head. He shook her hand, so you're the archaeologist, welcome to the building, Daniel must have mentioned us, Colette and Jacques Peyrelevade, but the name meant nothing to her. The woman gave her a kiss on the cheek, Hélène, the famous Hélène, she had a voice like a young woman's but she struggled to find her words, and her bun, like a loosening halyard, had let a hank of long white hair escape. They were thrilled because inside their mailbox they had just found a postcard with a magnificent image of the mountains of Patagonia, sent from Ushuaia, Daniel never forgot to write them, he sent a card on every trip. Hélène opened her mailbox, it was empty, she'd never received a postcard from her great-uncle, nor, as far as she knew, had any member of her family.

DANIEL WASN'T SEEN AT MANY ROCHE FAMILY REUNIONS because he spent part of the year traveling to the four corners of the world. On his rare visits, he would arrive late with unkempt hair and one end of his shirt collar poking out from his perennially crumpled and worn beige parka. When Hélène was a child, she was fascinated by that coat with its countless different-sized pockets, on the inside and the outside, even on the sleeves.

When Daniel did attend big family meals, he always sat at the children's table, far away from the adults. The kids begged him to tell stories, and he would embark on hare-brained tales of adventure, rolling his eyes, mimicking voices, accents, and animal calls, describing fantastical situations, stringing together puns and suddenly roaring with laughter when no one could quite see why. The crust of a baguette split in two became the jaws of a caiman chasing him through the muddy waters of the Orinoco, and he would stand up and mime swimming a crawl to get away. Or it was the middle of winter deep in the taiga, his lamp was about to go out, he was surrounded by howling wolves, and he stood his cutlery upright, quivering under his napkin like tent posts in a blizzard. The children's parents tried to get him to stop, can't you see you're scaring them, but he never listened and kept going on and on, for as long as the kids wanted him to. Hélène's brother laughed really loudly, but she knew she'd hear him talking in his sleep that night, he always did after these sessions.

At the end of the meal, Hélène's grandfather clinked his knife against his glass to get some quiet and said a few words in his resonant voice that was accustomed to reverberating around schoolyards. After that everyone started singing and the kids got down from the table. Left alone, Daniel sat in motionless silence, staring into space, occasionally touching his left breast pocket. Whatever the circumstances, he always wore shirts with buttoned pockets, and the left-hand one, which was invariably buttoned up, housed something the size of a cigarette case but it was impossible to guess anything more about it through the fabric.

SHE LEFT THE PEYRELEVADES IN THE ENTRANCE HALL with their postcard from Patagonia and went up to her room on the fifth floor. She undid her chignon, took off her high-heeled shoes, how she twisted her ankles in them, and walked about barefoot for the sheer pleasure of feeling the cool floor tiles. She'd soon got used to how small her room was, compensated as this was by the view over the Paris rooftops, and she really enjoyed being free to eat what she wanted when she wanted. In the evenings she lay on her bed resting her feet on the windowsill, with a bag of figs within reach, reading a book borrowed from the institute's library.

The only thing about the room that had bothered her at first was a framed reproduction hanging on the wall, a portrait of teenage girl in a white dress with a menorah behind her. In this black-and-white copy, which was probably smaller than the original, the image felt sinister, the girl's body was misshapen, her eyes startled, her fingers clutching hold of her knees. It was worst in the evening when the setting sun was reflected on the glass and set the dress ablaze so the girl appeared to be contorting amid the flames. The frame was nailed to the wall and so couldn't be taken down. After a few days, unable to look at it any longer, Hélène had taped a photo over it, a picture she'd torn from a magazine, of the earth from the air; and she'd thought no more of it.

3
The Giant Atlas

CLASSES AT THE INSTITUTE OF ARCHAEOLOGY had started at the beginning of October. At first Hélène felt sure the other students, who were older than her and already had three years' experience behind them, would be far more knowledgeable than she was. She had done only one training course, the previous summer, on a dig undertaken as a preventive measure under the metro station for the law courts in Toulouse, where a children's cemetery had been found. She was convinced this was no big deal and she listened in awe when her fellow students cited mysterious names, not even knowing if they were referring to people or places. She thought she'd be a beginner for the rest of her life. Strangely, though, this one experience proved quite a coup from their earliest conversations. She soon realized that a necropolis, particularly a children's cemetery, was to an apprentice architect what open-heart surgery was to a med student, a sort of initiation, it taught you as much as a whole string of courses.

Which was why one clique of students, which included Guillaume, soon accepted her as one of them. The first time they ate lunch together it was still warm enough to picnic in the Observatory Gardens opposite the institute building whose redbrick façade, with its diamond- and hexagon-shaped relief design, looked like something knitted by a giant. There were six of them, and they found a nice spot on the lawn, some lying full-length like Romans at a banquet, others sitting cross-legged like Egyptian scribes, all discussing their plans for the future. They had all chosen their specialties already: Egyptology, Latin paleography, Carolingian sculpture, Middle Eastern churches. And Hélène sat listening in silence.

But once they'd finished the meal and were getting to their feet, they turned into quite different people. Two girls started playing ping-pong with books and a ball of screwed-up paper. Guillaume used his plastic fork to dig a deep hole in the sandbox, pulling ecstatic faces every time he found so much as a blade of grass or the ring-pull from a beer can, and this made the others shriek with laughter. Hélène laughed along with them, but she wasn't sure it was funny.

Two days later she went to the institute's library to work on a presentation, and she was looking through an old large-format atlas which, once opened, was half the size of a bed. There was no way of seeing the top of the page without lying across the book. Someone sitting at a table nearby stood up and came over, and she recognized Guillaume. He leaned closer as he talked to her, you know, at the end of the room, there's a special counter for books this size, the giants of the book world, they're called Atlantic format. And before she could reply he'd taken the atlas over, and instead of sitting back down, he stayed there looking at the map she was working on and slowly traced the course of a river with his finger. These giant atlases were adventure books, once inside them you were traveling on paper, you just had to shrink, like Alice. She told him she didn't feel like it and, anyway, the Atlantic size books were making her seasick. She'd already noticed the way Guillaume tipped his head back when he laughed, making his Adam's apple stick out. Before he left, he sniffed the paper of the atlas, I love that smell, it smells of saffron, she shook her head, you're kidding, it stinks of old books. Later, when she knew Guillaume better, she still wondered how he turned everything he touched into a game.

4
Uncle Daniel

AS A CHILD, HÉLÈNE SOON WEARIED of her great-uncle's stories, of the endless performances he put on for the kids at family meals. His adventures were all the same — there were always storms, savage beasts, unscrupulous crooks, the same plot twists that salvaged hopeless situations just before the catastrophe. He unfailingly made himself the wiliest character, triumphing every time. When she was about eleven or twelve, she asked whether she could move up to the adults' table. From there she could still see Uncle Daniel, but she couldn't hear him, it was like someone had cut the sound track, which only made his gesticulations look all the more outlandish. She watched him cavorting about the room, with jerky mimed movements like a character in a silent movie. Her grandfather called him Charlie, and yes, there was something of Chaplin about Daniel.

Hélène had always felt that her great-uncle was somehow set apart from the family, and not only because of his curly hair and blue eyes. Her grandmother never said "my brother" when she talked about him, but she did say "my sister" for Aunt Paule. The Roches were sedentary types, bound for generations to their mountains in the Auvergne, even though some, like Hélène's father, had moved some distance away. Daniel, on the other hand, had itchy feet, he never stopped traveling. He was the only one who'd never married, but Hélène had heard her mother say it's a shame his clothes are such a mess because it's not like he's ugly. More significantly, though, the Roches had proper jobs, farming, midwifery, teaching, while Daniel had chosen a strange way to earn a crust: based on his travels abroad, he wrote adventure stories for children. Under the pseudonym H. R. Sanders, he wrote the *Black Insignia* series, which had been and still was very successful; it had been translated into several languages and adapted for film and television. On the back of each book were the words *Heart-stopping adventures where the hero battles his way through countless perils in far-flung lands and every imaginable climate, to ensure justice and truth win out.*

When Hélène moved to Paris, he was onto the twenty-third volume, but as far as the Roche family was concerned, twenty-three books was not enough to make a respectable man of Daniel. He might well live comfortably on the proceeds of his writing, but they saw it as, at best, a hobby, an amateur pursuit, Hélène's grandfather in particular said it was childish. He might have said the same of archaeology. He'd died in February that year, just before Hélène's twentieth birthday, and many years later she wondered whether, in her grandfather's lifetime, she would have dared throw herself into this Indiana Jones–style treasure hunt.

FOR HER TENTH BIRTHDAY AND HER BROTHER'S EIGHTH, Uncle Daniel had sent them a joint parcel containing the first four volumes of *The Black Insignia*. He carried on giving them subsequent volumes, one or two a year, as and when they were published, each with the same dedication, *For Hélène and Antoine, with all my affection, Daniel H. R.* The red-and-gray bindings gradually filled a bookcase in Antoine's bedroom. The boy devoured them. He was proud to be the author's great-nephew and felt invested with a form of responsibility, at school and in other situations. He showed the dedications to his friends and then, standing on chairs or hiding behind the sofa in the living room, they would reenact epic scenes in which they took turns playing Peter Ashley-Mill, his enemies and allies, in the ruins of Machu Picchu or the jungles of Borneo.

About twice a year Daniel visited them in Orléans and brought the children souvenirs from his travels. In the entrance hall, before taking off his beige parka, he would riffle through his myriad pockets, hamming up the

search like a clown and deliberately not finding their presents until he came to the last two pockets. For Antoine it was something different every time, the sloughed skin of a cobra, a baobab seed, an Egyptian papyrus; and for Hélène it was always a peculiar gemstone, and she never knew what to do with them. Her father kept her collection in a display case with labels: *Brazilian Aventurine, Ethiopian Amazonite, Bombay Scolecite, Madagascan Yellow Jasper.* He told her the stones were very valuable, you'll understand when you're older, but she thought her brother's presents were far more interesting.

At mealtimes Daniel spoke almost exclusively to Antoine, who asked him questions about Ashley-Mill's latest adventures, going back over such and such a detail. Hélène was convinced he wrote the stories for her brother, and she felt she might as well not have been there. At the first opportunity she would leave the room for fear that he would guess she wasn't interested in *The Black Insignia* and didn't want to know anything about it. She had started the first book in the series, *The Ferrymen of the Amazon*, and had made quite an effort to follow the wounded hero through the depths of the Amazon rain forest, but she'd given up before the end of the first chapter. She tried to persuade herself that they were stories for boys. Perhaps she was afraid she would have to plow through episodes that Daniel had given a test run, so to speak, at family gatherings. Mostly, though, she just felt too old to be taken in by all that eventful adventuring.

Truth be told, when Daniel came to Orléans he wasn't exactly the same as at big family parties. The cousins weren't around, there were just two children, and with this reduced audience he didn't show off so much. The adventures he talked about weren't his, anyway, they were his hero's, Peter Ashley-Mills. Unlike other relations, particularly Grandpa, Hélène's parents viewed Daniel with a degree of indulgence. Every now and then, without stopping what he was saying, he would touch his breast pocket, running his finger around the edge of the thing inside, the thing about the size of a cigarette case, as if to reassure himself it was still there. There were also strange, opaque words that cropped up in his conversation, like stones in a fast-flowing stream, words he was never heard to say at family gatherings but only when he was with them in Orléans. He never took the trouble to translate them, and Hélène imagined they were snatches of exotic languages brought back from his travels in distant lands.

5

The Anger of the Carinaua

JONAS'S LAST RITUAL ON HIS WALKS WITH HÉLÈNE in the
Luxembourg Gardens took place on the way home. Instead
of going straight to his apartment on the third floor, he
rang the bell on the second floor where Mrs. Peyrelevade
greeted him in her singsong voice, and he would run over
to a closet where they kept some old toys. He especially
liked a tiny camera, Ricordo di Napoli, not only for the
views of Naples but also for playing photographer. Mrs.
Peyrelevade would sit on the sofa, pull her skirt down over
her knees, and adopt a pose for him. One day that October
she turned to Hélène, on the subject of photos, there was
something she wanted to show her, she kept forgetting.
She took her into the bedroom. It was above the Empire-
style bed, in a mahogany frame, a photo of her wedding,
with fifteen or twenty people, look, my hair was absolutely black, you could see it where she'd lifted up her veil,
and there's my Jim, standing so tall, such a fine-looking
man. They were married in '41, sixty years in a couple of
years' time, can you believe that. Sitting cross-legged on

23

the ground in the front row were four little boys, three of them with neatly brushed hair, in short-sleeved shirts and white socks, but the fourth didn't look as if he was dressed for a wedding, with his striped knitted cardigan and that great chestnut brown curl lolling over his forehead. The old lady's thin hand trembled slightly on the edge of the frame, she seemed to be looking for something, scanning the faces again and again, particularly Jim's, but just then Jonas hurt himself and they went to console him.

IT RAINED THE NEXT DAY, and the students didn't picnic on the lawns of the Observatory Gardens. Hélène lived closer to the institute than any of the others so she suggested they take refuge in her apartment. The moment they were in her room, she regretted inviting them; there were six of them but it felt more like twenty people or that the walls had moved closer together. They sat all over the place, on her bed, on the chair, Guillaume sat on the floor, folding his long legs and wrapping his arms around them, like an Inca mummy.

It was always the same routine, they talked about archaeology until they'd finished their sandwiches, then they turned into kids again. They spread around the room, some opened books, others fiddled with pencils, or the knickknacks Hélène had brought from her parents'

24

house, things bought in flea markets when she'd developed a taste for vintage, a stuffed blue tit, an ashtray shaped like a skull, an iridescent ball of glass made to look like a soap bubble. In a way she was flattered they should take an interest in her humble treasures, but she was also worried seeing them manhandling these fragile things.

Two girls leaned on the windowsill to have a smoke, and they were so enthusiastic about the view that everyone else went over to look. Soon they were all kneeling on the bed, jostling to catch a glimpse of the Eiffel Tower. Only Guillaume carried on exploring the room, he was intrigued by the magazine page taped over the glass in the picture frame. Hélène peeled it off and he almost shouted I know that picture. It was Soutine's *Girl with Menorah*, he'd never seen it but had read a description of it in a novel. The people at the window turned around and a boy said yes, I remember, it's in *The Black Insignia*, it's about the war in the Lebanon, he couldn't remember the title. Guillaume knew, though, it was in *Of Milk, Honey, and Powder*. Spotting this same picture hanging on the only wall left standing in a bombed house, Peter Ashley-Mill recognizes the painter's style, having met the man when he was a child. Interestingly, it was the only passage in the whole series that mentioned Peter's childhood.

Conversations gradually bubbled up around the room, interconnecting and overlapping. They'd all read several

stories in *The Black Insignia*, some even the whole series, they remembered every book, who'd given it to them, the characters they'd liked, the little beggar girl who climbed up a skyscraper to free her father in *Kidnapped in Bombay*, the rag-and-bone kid in Cairo who saved his sister in *The Scarab of Henouttaneb*, or the Chinese peasant woman who found a terra-cotta soldier at the bottom of a well, and especially of course Peter, the lone adventurer they'd all fallen for, blundering and absentminded but managing to foil every trap and never failing to save the downtrodden of this world. The girl who specialized in Latin epigraphs had even drawn her hero's tattoo onto her arm with a felt pen.

Hélène didn't say anything, all these names, Itsme, Ahyam, Mi Yu, reminded her of her brother's childhood games, and she was amazed to hear students, at their age, talking about these characters as if they'd met them yesterday. They couldn't agree about *The Ferrymen of the Amazon*, the first book. Guillaume couldn't see that the anger of the Carinaua people was justified, they'd saved Peter, the old cacique Umoro even called him my son, and out of nowhere, for no obvious reason, they tied him to a canoe and sent him across the river, threatening to kill him if he ever came back. Hélène's friends tried to find an explanation, perhaps the Indians wanted to protect their forests, knowing intuitively that a white man might betray them, but Guillaume refused to accept that Peter was a traitor. They were all there in her bedroom talking so loudly that, to quiet them down, Hélène tried to tell them that her great-uncle had written the books, but her voice got lost in the racket and no one heard her.

THAT EVENING SHE FOUND A POSTCARD OF PATAGONIA in her mailbox. It was sent from Ushuaia, featured low-slung houses against a background of mountains, and had a really beautiful stamp. She recognized her great-uncle's handwriting, the same writing as those dedications in the *Black Insignia* books, its sloping letters clinging to each other with tiny connecting hooks as if afraid of losing each other. *My dear Hélène, I hope you've settled into rue Vavin. It's magnificent here. I'll tell you all about it, but only if you insist ... Affectionately, Daniel H. R.*

6
A Shambles

ON OCTOBER 24, exactly a month after Hélène arrived in Paris, Uncle Daniel returned from his travels, as his neighbors had said he would. She was leaning out her window smoking that evening and spotted him crossing the courtyard, which was already almost completely dark. He was heading to the shed with a particularly heavy-looking garbage bag. From above he looked shorter, a balding patch showed on the top of his head, and his back had become slightly stooped since the last time she'd seen him. Not knowing he was being watched, he didn't have his usual alert, springing gait, but walked heavily, as if he were tired.

Hélène had never known Daniel's true age. She knew he was the youngest of the three Roche children, and she never wondered why, unlike his sisters, there were no pictures of him as a tiny baby in family albums. He first appeared in a photo of the Saint-Ferréol boys' school, his hair cropped short, wearing a smock and clogs, surrounded by other schoolboys. His life started with that image.

As she emerged from childhood she had eventually asked her father why Daniel hadn't been taken to a photographer as a baby, as his sisters had. Her father had run his hand over his face, he wasn't taken because he wasn't born into the family, he came to Saint-Ferréol during the war, he was an orphan and the Roches took him in and then later adopted him. To her ears, the words *war* and *orphan* formed a quite natural pair, wars kill parents, no need to picture how it actually happens, and she glossed over the missing episode in the same way that, as a child, she used to skip the page where the mother dies in the book about Babar the elephant.

This revelation explained why she'd always thought of Daniel as a sort of foreign body in the family. Perhaps it was also why he carried on behaving like a child, as if he'd stopped growing up when he came to the Roches, as if he was ten years old forever. And, with all the wisdom of her eleven years, she'd felt older than him. She still found it odd that he'd so completely forgotten his first parents that he never talked about them, and to test the experience for herself she erased her own parents' faces in her mind, but the harder she tried to do it, the more clearly they appeared to her behind her closed eyelids.

She'd learned later, from her grandfather, that his name was originally Daniel Ascher, he was Jewish, Grandpa added, drawing out the sibilant end of the word.

Apart from these few snatches of information, neither Daniel himself nor any other member of the family had ever mentioned his origins, and she surmised that it wasn't right to ask questions for fear of twisting goodness knows what sort of knife in goodness knows what sort of wound. She knew nothing and wanted to know nothing about Daniel's former life, his parents or his brothers and sisters, if he had any. That story doesn't belong to this family's memories, as her grandfather used to say, it was none of their business.

WHEN HÉLÈNE CAME HOME FROM THE INSTITUTE the day after Daniel's return, she found a note slipped under the door to her room: *I arrived home from Tierra del Fuego yesterday, I brought you back a little souvenir. Come over one of these days, whatever time suits you, but I won't be too flavorsome in the mornings because of the thyme difference*, another one of his dumb word games. She didn't like the thought of him climbing all the way up to her floor and, to be sure he didn't come back, she decided to visit him the very next day.

Daniel's apartment was on the ground floor and had a separate entrance in the hallway. Hélène struck the lion's head knocker for a long time before he opened the door. She'd visited his apartment only once, as a child, when

she was eight or nine, and the place had felt like some sort of fascinating museum, full of things brought home from far-flung countries, things she could never have imagined ending up here. She remembered a rhinoceros skull with its bluish horn, Inca statuettes in terra-cotta, three grimacing African masks, a stuffed alligator on the mantelpiece in the living room, a tiger skin on the floor, with glass eyes and jaws open to show varnished teeth, but most of all, the thing that had kind of hypnotized her and her brother, the shrunken head of a Jivaroan Indian with long black hair and lips carefully stitched shut.

There were probably more artifacts in the apartment now, but the tiger skin was shedding its hair, the rhinoceros skull was covered in dust, and the alligator above the fireplace looked like a big lizard. As a child she hadn't noticed how untidy and dirty the place was, and now it just looked like an ill-lit shambles, cluttered with piles of books, papers, and half-opened maps.

Daniel was wearing a poncho over his shirt, he kissed her exuberantly, you've grown again, she was taller than him now, come on in, I'll make you a coffee, it's coffee time. She didn't really feel like it but followed him into the kitchen, the sink was full of dirty dishes, I'm really sorry, I didn't have time yet to do the dishes, it was obvious they'd been waiting there since before he left. He put the coffee-maker on the stove to heat, and washed two mismatched cups, he hadn't had time to buy sugar since he came home either, he'd do better next time, or actually he'd invite her to a restaurant, on a Sunday. She thought it wouldn't be too much of a shame if he forgot.

As she went along the corridor back to the living room, she caught sight of a detail she'd noticed on her previous visit but had forgotten. It was a large brown suitcase lying on the floor near the bed, a case so heavy that between the two of them she and her brother hadn't succeeded in lifting it off the floor, they'd wanted to open it but their parents had called them back to the living room, it's bad manners going into people's bedrooms like that. She remembers picturing Daniel hunched under this weighty load as he walked the pathways of the world.

The bookcase in the living room was so full you couldn't have added one more volume. There was hardly any furniture, just a TV and a large desk, and fixed to the edge of the desk was a pencil sharpener with a crank handle. Books and atlases were piled up on the desk. An old Michelin map of France was open, cut across by a red line drawn in felt pen, and scattered with desk pads and notebooks filled with lists and complicated diagrams in which the words *ferryman* and *boat* had been circled. On the cover of a thick exercise book were a number of deleted titles, *The First*, *The Last Voyage of*, *The Refuge of*, *Return to Home Base*. Images of planets scrolled across the computer screen. A glass filled with finely sharpened pencils stood next to the screen.

Daniel brought the coffee through to the living room and moved a pile of newspapers off the only armchair so that Hélène could sit down, and he himself sat in the desk chair. He was near the window and in that light she thought he looked even more tired than he had in the courtyard the previous evening. His hair was going white, he'd shrunk slightly, and he looked faintly ridiculous with his poncho whose fringes had gotten wet in the kitchen. He sat there looking at her in silence for a moment, his eyes alighting on her hair, her eyes, her shoulders, and she was a little embarrassed. It was the first time in her life she'd been alone with him.

He asked jokingly whether she was finding it too windy up there in her crow's nest, he inquired about her studies at the Institute of Archaeology, if he'd been able to study, that's what he would have chosen, but he hadn't even bothered to take his secondary-school exams. He didn't talk about his trip, she was the one who ended up asking, so then, how was Tierra del Fuego. And all of a sudden, as if she'd set in motion some mechanical device, he became animated, he started talking faster, describing how his car broke down in the middle of nowhere, how his suitcase got mixed up with someone else's on the stopover in Buenos Aires, he mimicked the Aerolineas employee falling over himself apologizing, *lo sentimos mucho*, gesticulating like a child, over the top, as usual. And yet, even at this point, Hélène felt something about him had changed, not just his graying hair, something more than that, perhaps his eyes, the expression in them. She struggled to finish her unsweetened coffee, it was so bitter.

In the hallway when she was leaving, Daniel took his parka off its hook to retrieve something from one of the pockets, a small object wrapped in tissue paper, for you, a little souvenir, it was a stone, obviously, blood red with flesh-colored veining, a Tierra del Fuego agate. Then, at the very last minute, he almost whispered, you know, you remind me so much of my sister, and he closed the door very quickly. People often told Hélène she looked like her grandmother, especially her almond-shaped eyes. She knew Suzanne was Daniel's favorite sister.

7
Wielding an Axe

IT WASN'T ACTUALLY BOREDOM that had made Hélène give up on *The Ferrymen of the Amazon*. The scant chapter she'd once read, a dozen or so pages, had made her feel short of breath, stifling under some burden. The story began with a catastrophe: a twin-engine plane flying over the Amazon rain forest stalls and crashes into the trees. The pilot and two photographers are killed, Peter Ashley-Mill is the only survivor. Despite deep wounds to his arm and chest, he manages to find the strength, wielding an axe, to hack his way through the climbers and giant trees, not sure whether he will find any humans, or how they will receive him. Starving, hunched, and in pain, he battles on, sometimes resting his hand on the oozing wound close to his heart, under his torn shirt. When he is collapsing with hunger, he digs up roots. Even though the parrots taunt him, *You're going to die, Peter, you're going to die*, he holds on, determined to survive at all costs so he can report the tragic deaths of his companions. But overcome by exhaustion, pain, and fever, he loses consciousness.

A huge anaconda eases down from a branch and slowly wraps itself around his body.

She didn't get any farther, but the story haunted her all through her teenage years, she still sometimes dreamed that she was fighting through a hostile jungle, plying her way through the tree trunks and climbers, digging into the ground to find roots, to no avail.

WITH THE LATE OCTOBER RAINS, the students abandoned their outpost in the Observatory Gardens and withdrew to the Café des Facultés on the corner of rue Joseph Bara. Between lectures, they sat around a table in the cavernous back room, which was often almost empty in the afternoons. One day when all the others had left, Hélène and Guillaume found themselves alone together. He was trying to scoop the dregs of his hot chocolate from the bottom of his cup, and she sat watching him bring his spoon up to his mouth. That was when she admitted, you know, H. R. Sanders is my great-uncle. And she almost immediately wondered whether she'd done the right thing.

The spoon stopped on the edge of Guillaume's lips, he looked up at her, what, who did you say, yes, H. R. Sanders, he's my great-uncle. He looked at her for a long time, scrutinizing her face, her hair, the collar of her jacket, as if looking for proof, a similarity between her and Peter

Ashley-Mill, I thought Sanders was American, and as he said *American*, he spread his arms wide to encompass the great expanses of the Far West. I swear it's true. He couldn't understand why she hadn't mentioned it in the early days when they'd all talked about *The Black Insignia*.

Then, just as Jonas would have done, he said, go on, then, tell me what's he like. She'd never had to describe her great-uncle, of course she could keep quiet about his eccentricities and his collar all askew, but if she was going to paint a flattering portrait she would have to borrow the words her neighbors had used, like *brave*, *valiant*, *tireless*, and she wasn't up to that. She just explained that H. R. Sanders was a nom de plume, that his real name was Daniel Roche, Guillaume repeated the name, Daniel Roche, and she could tell he was disappointed, it was too ordinary, too sedentary. She had to give more details, for example telling him that he lived in the same building as her on rue Vavin, that it was Roche who'd lent her the garret room. Guillaume put down his spoon and ran a hand through his hair. At last he believed her, she was H. R. Sanders's great-niece, he looked at her affectionately, almost reverently. Could he bring his *Black Insignia* books over to her place so she could ask him to write dedications in them, or even, he lowered his voice, could he meet him? She hesitated, these were two different, irreconcilable worlds, and the sight of Daniel Roche, kind of short and slight with his unkempt hair and his gesticulating, would do even less for Guillaume than his real name had. She said he was traveling, but Guillaume was already leaning over the table and kissing her cheek to thank her, as if she were the go-between for an enraptured lover.

8
The Black Insignia

GUILLAUME WENT TO HIS PARENTS' HOUSE over the long weekend at Halloween and picked up his twenty-three volumes of *The Black Insignia*, then he came and dropped them with Hélène in a big sports bag. It was the first time they were at her place alone. He looked out the window at the waves of gray rooftops glistening with rain, like an ocean seen through a porthole, you could even hear seagulls crying. Hélène pointed at the windows on the ground floor overlooking the courtyard, H. R. Sanders lived there.

The books in the bag were definitely the same ones as on her brother's bookshelves, but dog-eared and held together with tape, and they looked less intimidating in this state. Guillaume picked up the oldest, the most battered of all, on the cover was a picture of Peter bound hand and foot in a canoe and, at either end, an Indian paddling through the eddies and caimans of the Amazon. Why do the Carinaua suddenly drive Peter out, you know the author well, you must know why. She didn't want to admit that she'd only read the first few pages, afraid he might

lose that affectionate look he'd had in his eyes recently. She said I've forgotten why, it was so long ago, maybe he did something wrong, offended their moral code or their beliefs, but Guillaume disagreed. She would read it again, while the book was with her, before she handed the series over to Daniel.

SHE KEPT PUTTING OFF THE MOMENT to introduce Guillaume to her great-uncle, persuading herself she should at least finish *The Ferrymen of the Amazon*, but the bag stayed zipped up in the corner of her room. The meeting happened without her, by chance, one afternoon in mid-November, when she was taking Jonas home after a walk in the Luxembourg Gardens and Guillaume was waiting in the entrance hall. When she came back downstairs, he'd gone, the door to the cellar was open, and she could hear voices drifting up. The stairs down to the cellar were badly lit, the switch didn't work, she felt her way with her hands on the walls. Guillaume was down there, at the end of a long dark corridor, with the caretaker, Mrs. Almeida, and Daniel, who was training a flashlight on an electric meter; they were talking about fuses and cutouts. She'd never ventured into the basement, the place looked older than the building above, with vaulted ceilings, a beaten earth floor, and a musty, underground smell. The power cut was complicated, they'd have to call an electrician. By the time Hélène joined them, they were turning back toward the stairs, following Daniel, who lit the way for them. At one point, the beam of his flashlight lit up a side corridor whose walls were not made of the same stone but of cinder blocks, but just as Hélène stepped forward for a closer look, Daniel snapped the flashlight away and, finding she was in darkness, Hélène hurried to catch up with the others.

When she reemerged into the hallway, Daniel was talking to Guillaume, who was leaning toward him and laughing very loudly. From the look of them you'd have thought they'd known each other for years. Of course they were talking about *The Black Insignia*, Guillaume was using exaggerated words like *admirer*, *passionate*, *devoted*. He remembered as a teenager going to a bookshop in Marseille where H. R. Sanders was meant to be doing a book signing, but he'd waited in vain, the event was eventually canceled, I'm so sorry, I must have been traveling. Guillaume went up to get his books from Hélène's room and came back all out of breath from racing up and down the stairs so quickly. Seeing Guillaume with his enormous sports bag, Daniel started laughing, are they all in there, yes, all twenty-three, they're all battered, I've read them so many times, I know them by heart. Daniel opened the bag and took out a few books, how wonderful, the broken spines, the stains and scars, it's what every writer dreams of. He invited them both for coffee on the last Saturday of the month, he winked at Hélène, don't worry, I've bought some sugar. Guillaume said goodbye to Daniel, calling him Mr. Sanders, Hélène nearly corrected him, but Daniel looked delighted and clasped Guillaume's hand in both of his for a long time, until next time, my dear, my very dear reader, until next time.

THEY WENT UP TO HER ROOM, and the corner where the bag had been suddenly looked strangely empty. They shared a packet of biscuits, and Guillaume broke several before they reached his mouth, his hands were shaking slightly, he was still all flustered from meeting the author of *The Black Insignia*. Hélène was lucky, he'd have liked a great-uncle like that, she nodded and said there's something I have to admit to you, promise you won't hate me, he put his hand on his heart, I promise. She'd never read Sanders's books, she'd never got beyond the third chapter of *The Ferrymen of the Amazon*. Guillaume gulped down half a biscuit, you're kidding, tell me you're kidding, she shook her head, laughing so much it brought tears to her eyes.

She really knew nothing about the books. She didn't even know why the series was called *The Black Insignia*, some sort of death threat maybe, like pirates have, no, not at all, I'll explain, the insignia is a talisman, a shamanic

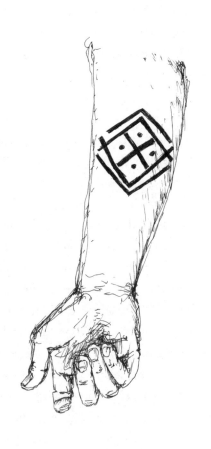

tattoo, it can protect you from danger but also help you cross into the hereafter. In the most perilous episodes in every book, the insignia reminded Peter he'd brushed with death and it had saved him, and it would give him the strength to continue his battle against the adversities and injustices of this world. It didn't appear until the fourth chapter of the first book, he could tell her the story.

They sat down on the floor facing each other, Hélène leaning against her bed, and Guillaume the desk. Sitting with his hands open as if he were holding the book, he started reciting the opening sentences, *It was a very bad sign. The pilot was quite sure of it, the note of the engine had changed, and the plane was losing altitude.* Hélène stopped Guillaume, he could skip the first three chapters and pick up the story where she'd left off, where Peter has passed out and is about to be throttled by an anaconda.

An arrow drives through the snake's head. Members of the Carinaua, a completely isolated tribe, save Peter's life. They carry him, still unconscious, to the hut of their sha-man, Yomi. When Peter comes around several days later, Yomi's remedies have already healed his wounds. He finds his left forearm has been tattooed with a wide bracelet design of geometric shapes, as worn by all the men in the tribe. He regains his strength, the Indians teach him their language, and the old cacique Umoro treats him like his own son. And then all of a sudden, with no explanation,

47

their faces harden, they blindfold Peter, bind him hand and foot on a canoe, and send him across the Amazon, which is as wide as an ocean. Umoro stands on the bank for a long time, bow in hand, full of menace, as if Peter might throw himself into the waters and swim back. The hero continues on his way, reaches a town, and discovers that he was believed dead. Doctors describe the way his wounds have healed as miraculous, a major pharmaceuticals company finances an expedition to locate the Carinaua and their mysterious remedy. Out of love for mankind, Peter agrees to be their guide, but the team's arrogance makes him change his mind and, when they're close to their goal, he slips away to warn the Indians. As he draws near to the village, trying to remember friendly words of greeting in the Carinaua language, an arrow whistles past his neck and plants itself in his backpack.

Guillaume looked up to read the effects of the suspense on Hélène's face. She got to her feet, she didn't want to hear any more.

9
A Block of Soap

THE FOLLOWING SATURDAY, Hélène spotted Daniel talking to the man from the hardware store on his doorstep on rue Bréa. Since Daniel's return she'd often come across him in the neighborhood, he was never alone, perhaps drinking mint tea in the little grocery, or enjoying a Japanese beer with the florist in front of her display, or having lunch on a café terrace with a homeless person. He seemed to know them all, was on first-name terms with the shopkeepers, patted them on the shoulder, joked with them, he was almost always the one doing most of the talking, probably telling them about his latest travels. She felt he overdid it, as usual, gesticulating, making a fool of himself. She tried to make sure he didn't see her but wasn't always successful.

On this particular day she couldn't avoid him, he introduced her to the man from the hardware store, his old friend Louis, you mean your long-standing friend, I'm no older than you are, don't you forget we were classmates at school. Louis, heavy and almost completely bald, looked much older than Daniel, and it took her a while to grasp that this wasn't a joke, that the school they were talking about was one Daniel had attended in early childhood, back in the beginning, before Saint-Ferréol. He was a troublemaker, young Daniel, the shopkeeper went on, the teacher gave him sentences to write and detentions, but it was no good, that's not true, you're getting it all mixed up, old boy, you were the one who was on the wild side. But Louis was on a roll, your mother used to send you here when my parents ran the store, you'd come over from rue Delambre to buy Marseille soap, and afterward you'd tell her you'd lost the change.

This reminded Hélène of a time when, without her parents seeing, Daniel had slipped a ten-franc coin into her hand, then put a finger to his lips, she must have been eight years old. She'd hidden the coin deep in her pocket like a thief, thrilled and guilt-ridden in equal measure, and then she'd forgotten about it, the jeans had gone through the wash and the coin had disappeared.

Daniel was laughing and coughing at the same time, my poor Louis, you're losing your memory, I didn't live on rue Delambre but on rue d'Odessa, oh yes, you're right, it was rue d'Odessa, but you didn't give the change back all the same. Daniel looked down and, as if talking to himself, he repeated *rue d'Odessa*. Louis didn't notice and carried on talking, do you remember there were hookers on rue Delambre in those days, they've all gone now, the

neighborhood store's shut up shop, my friend, he guffawed but Daniel looked embarrassed.

As Hélène headed toward the intersection, she pictured a very young boy, not much bigger than Jonas, she could see him crossing boulevard du Montparnasse beside her, carrying a great block of soap, hurrying to get home to his mother. Rue d'Odessa. She knew vaguely where that was, over toward the metro station, Odessa, that's a name you don't forget. But of the road itself, she remembered nothing at all.

10

Sanders's Bookcase

THE FOLLOWING SATURDAY AFTERNOON, they went to have tea with Daniel. Before they set off, Guillaume had paced around and around Hélène's room like a little kid. The door to Daniel's apartment was ajar, come on, you can come on in, they found him in the living room playing chess, I'd like to introduce my great friend Sadi Alfa Maneh, known as Prosper. The man's gray hair formed a sort of cloud in the light from the window. Hélène apologized for interrupting their game, they'd come back later, but Daniel and his friend insisted they stay, Prosper had to go anyway, they were used to interrupted games of chess. Prosper took two visiting cards from his jacket pocket and handed them one each: *Monsieur Maneh, great African marabout, solves all your problems in love, friendship, and work, facilitates the return of a loved one, as well success in exams and driving tests. Peerless specialist in love letters. Satisfaction or your money back. By appointment.* Now, young man, I really am an expert with love letters, I have a wonderful way with words, if you'd like to write one to this young lady, then I could give you a special rate, and for you, Hélène, as a relation of Daniel's, the consultation would be free, you'd be welcome to come and see me whenever you like at 36 rue de la Goutte d'Or. Remember that address, Daniel added with a laugh, it may come in handy, you never know.

When Prosper had left, Daniel explained that he'd first met him as a garbageman, clinging to the handle of a garbage truck, a real king of the blacktop who called himself Prosper like in that old song by Maurice Chevalier, and Daniel started singing it, beating out the time with his hand. Hélène felt herself blushing for her great-uncle. He and Prosper had had so many early-morning encounters they'd eventually got to know each other, and Prosper had slipped off his encrusted glove to shake hands. Daniel had offered to comb through the litter with him, and they'd made some wonderful finds together, what sort of finds, Guillaume asked, but Daniel didn't seem to hear the question. They'd gradually become friends and had told each other their childhood memories, between them they'd done every sort of job, courier, soldier, dockworker, typesetter, driver, cook. Prosper ended up as a marabout, in other words a sort of African psychoanalyst, if you see what I mean, the answer is always in the patient's question.

Guillaume was walking around the room like someone visiting a museum, and recognizing things from the *Black*

Insignia books, the African masks reminded him of *All the Honey in Casamance*, the Inca statuettes and the shrunken head of *The Curse of Machu Picchu*, and the stuffed alligator of *Terror on the Orinoco*. There were only two brief mentions in the whole series of Peter's home, his refuge, readers didn't even know which country it was in, but Guillaume had pictured it exactly like this, a stopping-off point, a nomad's brief resting place, transient, with nothing really settled.

Before he drank his coffee, he wanted to read Daniel's dedications, *To Guillaume, the enthusiastic reader*, *To Guillaume, the perceptive reader*, he found a different adjective in each book and was quite overwhelmed. Then he ferreted through the bookcase, Daniel showed him a few of the many translations of his books, *Pe drumul spre Transilvania*, *Aunt Lucy's Cabin*, *L'America o la muerte*. He took out various rarities such as editions of the popular children's magazine *Spirou* featuring *The Forsaken of Myanmar* in cartoon form. There were also live-action and animated film adaptations of *The Black Insignia*, Guillaume knew them, but in his view, nothing measured up to the books. Daniel conceded that they were disappointing, that's what a lot of readers think. For fun, he put a video on to show Guillaume the beginning of a Japanese animation of *For a Handful of Pearls*, as yet unseen in Europe, but Guillaume refused to recognize Peter in the blond-locked, martial-arts-performing teenager, what a betrayal. Hélène had moved over to the window, enjoying all the goings-on in the street that she couldn't see from her room because it overlooked the courtyard.

While they had their coffee, with sugar this time, Guillaume asked when the next *Black Insignia* book would be published. Daniel spread his hands, he was working on it, it would be finished in the spring, he'd kept his readers waiting longer than usual but this book would be special, unlike any of the others, it would be about the hero's younger days. It was set in several countries, in fact he was planning another trip, before Christmas he was off to Mauritania for six weeks, a magnificent country, he was going to see the famous decorative entrances in Oualata, and meet some Haratines, descended from slaves; he showed Guillaume his itinerary on the map. He wanted to speak out about children killed or injured along the route of the Paris–Dakar rally, kids whose parents were compensated with a only few dollars. This was the first time Hélène had heard him talk in such a serious, level-headed way, not putting on his usual performance, it was as if, for Guillaume's sake, he wanted to be on a par with Ashley-Mill, the dispenser of justice, the savior of the downtrodden. She noticed that when Guillaume listened to Daniel he sometimes peered at her great uncle's left forearm, as if hoping to see a tattoo peeping out from his shirtsleeve.

Just before they left, Daniel did manage to play the fool with the sneakers he'd recently bought for walking through the Sahara, on the box were the words *Just do it*, I could make that my motto. Guillaume congratulated him, these were the latest style with air bubbles in the soles, and Daniel put them on and flitted around the room, this is great, now I'm like the poet Rimbaud, the man with soles of wind.

THE FOLLOWING TUESDAY when he arrived home from his walk, Jonas stopped at the Peyrelevades' apartment as usual. Colette had gone out to do some shopping, so it was her husband, Jim, who opened the door. Jonas ran off to find the toy cars and drove them in and out under the fringe on the armchair. Jim managed to walk through the apartment without the help of a walking stick and turned to Hélène to ask whether she'd seen the photo of her great-uncle. She didn't know what he meant, you'll like this, Colette wanted to show it to you but she must have forgotten, she's losing her memory a bit. He went off to the bedroom to get a large envelope with a photograph inside it. It was the same picture of their wedding, only not so faded by sunlight, my word, we were young in '41, Colette was twenty-two, look, there he is, in the front row. He put his finger on the fourth child, sitting cross-legged and wearing a dark cardigan. It was definitely the boy with the long eyelashes from the Saint-Ferréol class photo, just with a slightly fuller face, slightly longer hair, and a smile. Jim showed her a stamp in the bottom right-hand corner, which didn't appear on the other copy, *Studio Ascher, photography, 16 rue d'Odessa, Paris XIVe*. Against the advice of their parents, especially Colette's, he and Colette had particularly wanted Mr. Ascher to photograph them, and to put his stamp on the picture, even though he'd been forced to remove his name from his sign. He'd brought his son along with him, Daniel was nine at the time and so small he had to climb on a stool to hold the flash.

Hélène understood why she hadn't recognized Daniel right away when Colette had shown her the picture. He was the schoolboy from Saint-Ferréol and yet he was another child, not just because of his plump cheeks and curls, but also there was something different about the look in his eyes. Jim was still talking, it was Colette who wanted him to join in the photo, my father-in-law sulked, look, but you can't refuse the bride anything. We had to supply the paper for the prints, Mr. Ascher couldn't get hold of it anymore, he chose to believe things wouldn't go on like that, a brave sort. His wife was from Poland, too, she had a strong accent, stronger than his, she used to touch up the photos, had a gift for it, I watched her working with a perfectly sharpened pencil, sharp as a scalpel, she could shape an oval face better than a plastic surgeon, her husband used to joke that she'd have made a great counterfeiter. The Aschers were good friends with Chaim Soutine, and he also used to touch up photos, when he was a young man in Vilna. Mr. Ascher used to go to his studio at Villa Seurat to photograph his paintings.

Jim Peyrelevade explained that they'd had Daniel to stay in the summer of 1942, you must have heard about that, he was here for nearly three weeks, hiding in this apartment, reading masses of books and children's magazines, *Treasure Island*, Bayard boys' magazines, while he waited for them to find a way to evacuate him to the free zone. The old man put the photo back into the envelope, and the envelope in its file. Daniel looks so like his father, every time I see him I can't help thinking about Mr. Ascher, what a story that was, oh my Lord, what a story, still, I don't know why I'm telling you all this, you know more about it than I do.

11

Under the Pirate's Watchful Eye

HÉLÈNE ASKED GUILLAUME if he would come to rue d'Odessa with her to see the house where H. R. Sanders had spent his childhood, she rather dreaded the idea of going on her own and felt that, if need be, Guillaume's enthusiasm would save her from becoming too maudlin. It was an ordinary, fairly short street, the kind you get near railroad stations, with hotels, restaurants, and people in a hurry. They set off from Place du 18-juin-1940 and tried to find where the Ascher Studio would have been. But number 16 had disappeared. There was a gap in the sequence of houses between 14 and 20. A new apartment building stretched across this gap, a little way back from the sidewalk, wide with balconies in smoked glass. They stood there, the two of them, in front of that building, looking to left and right, hoping they'd got the address wrong. This structure clearly occupied the space of the old numbers 16 and 18. Is this some kind of joke or something? Guillaume wailed, they've stolen H. R. Sanders's house, but when he saw Hélène's face he quieted down and put an arm around her shoulder, like a rescuer wrapping a blanket around the numbed body of a survivor.

They walked along rue d'Odessa to boulevard Edgar Quinet, Daniel's house was the only one that had been knocked down. Hélène wondered whether some of the shops had already been there at the time, the baker, or the furrier, perhaps. Yes, this street was definitely dreary, its window displays joyless despite the Christmas decorations hanging here and there. It was a far cry from Odessa, the splendor of old Russia and the sun glittering on the Black Sea.

Boulevard Edgar Quinet was bustling with life and noise, it was market day, Guillaume bought some caramelized peanuts, tossing them in the air and catching them in his mouth to make Hélène laugh. He showed her that if you kept looking at the top of the Montparnasse tower as you walked, you felt like it was falling toward you. She tried for a few seconds, grabbing hold of Guillaume to keep her balance, jostling a few passersby, it really was a childish game and she was a little ashamed of making a spectacle of herself.

SHE'D PROMISED JONAS she would take him to the puppet show in the Luxembourg Gardens that afternoon to watch *The Wolf and the Seven Young Kids*, and Guillaume went

along with them. The puppets must have been around for the best part of a century, and the wolf's dusty moth-eaten black fur made his huge bared red jaws look even more terrifying. When his violent hammering rattled the door to the cottage, the children gave their first screams of terror and delight. From where she was sitting in the back row with Guillaume, Hélène could see Jonas's tousled head bobbing about right at the front, with the youngest children. The wolf came back and waggled one of his white paws, and the audience screamed louder, no, don't open the door, it's the wolf. And when he swallowed up six of the kids one by one, cackling with pleasure, some of the children started to cry and ran to their parents' arms, but Jonas, fascinated, stayed where he was. Hélène took Guillaume's hand. The floor of the little theater, reverberating to the children's shouting and stamping, was shuddering beneath her feet.

Inside the ransacked cottage, the goat was weeping for her kids, unaware that the last one was hiding inside the clock case. Hélène turned toward Guillaume and their lips touched briefly. The emergency exit was just behind them, they snuck outside, she hesitated for a moment, you must be crazy, what about Jonas. It was already dark and it was raining so they ran, skirting around the building to a green metal door that led to the theater store in the backstage area. The door was ajar and they went inside into a room as tall and narrow as a tower and filled with scenery flats, accessories, and dozens of puppets hung at various heights in the gloom. They were just behind the stage and, on the far side of the painted fabric backdrop, they could see the puppeteers' feet and their shadows moving. The voices sounded louder than in the auditorium, *mommy, his stomach's moving, they're alive*, the scissors snapped horribly as they opened up the wolf's stomach while the children clapped deliriously.

Hélène and Guillaume leaned against a seascape with towering turquoise waves crashing onto rocks. Their mouths drew together, and the back of Guillaume's neck felt as soft as a child's against Hélène's hand. Just above them, a pirate's one good eye bulged at them, Guillaume took hold of the puppet's beard and turned him to face the other way. Only yards away, the kid goats were coming back to life one by one, *My little ones, let's put rocks in his stomach and stitch him back up*, then they sang and danced a triumphant dance, which Hélène and Guillaume would have liked to go on much longer. When they returned to the theater, the audience was already leaving and a panic-stricken Jonas was looking for them everywhere.

GUILLAUME SAID HIS GOODBYES TO THEM outside their building, and Hélène stayed with Jonas until his mother came home. When she reached the top of the back staircase, she found Guillaume sitting outside her door with his arms around his knees, laughing to see her surprise. He was a stowaway asking for asylum in her cabin for the night. Once on board her bedroom, he started staggering, the sea was rough and the swell threw him into Hélène's arms, help, be quiet, stop being so silly, she put her lips to his mouth. She'd already known a few boys, short-lived encounters that had mostly left an impression of haste and clumsiness. What she was now discovering was quite different. She agreed to go along with the game, for now.

12

Odessa Passage

FROM THEN ON, Hélène and Guillaume ended up alone together almost every evening, and he sometimes spent the night with her. It was always him coming to rue Vavin; he rented a room in an apartment in Montrouge and his land-lady didn't allow visitors. He left a few clothes in Hélène's room and she liked having them there when he wasn't around. Even so, he didn't know that she'd gone back to rue d'Odessa a week after they went there together. There really had to be some vestige of the past, a trace of Daniel's house, and she needed to be on her own to find it. Despite his passion for *The Black Insignia* and H. R. Sanders, Guillaume didn't seem to get Daniel's personal story.

She left quite early on the Saturday morning, deter-mined to spend as long as it took to dig up something, patiently, meticulously, just like an archaeologist. She walked the length of the street very steadily, looking at every level of the buildings from the ground to the roof, and she eventually found a detail on the stone façade of number 5, a blue-and-white sign bearing the strange inscription STEAM BATHS, and over the door were the words ODESSA BATHS. There was no code needed or entry phone, so she was able to cut across the hall to the inner courtyard. What confronted her was an oriental prince's folly, transported here as if by magic. The bathhouse was entirely covered in tiles in every color of the sea, it was decorated with large mascarons over the windows, and the blue and green tiles on the dados mimicked streaming water. She could now see why the street bore the sumptuous faraway name of Odessa. She wondered whether the Ascher family had had their own bathroom, or had used these former public baths, but what little knowledge she had of their lives provided no answers.

After those colorful tiles, the dirty, gray, brown-stained façade of the 16–18 building was sad enough to make her weep. What really upset her, she would come to realize much later, wasn't the building itself, which was very ordinary, but the fact that it had been built on the ruins of Daniel's house. In the center of the apartment building, a gate of closely spaced metal bars stood half open. A dark gallery, like a sort of subway corridor, led away behind it, and at the far end was a peep of light as if from a basement window. The ceiling was very low and covered in vertical strips of metal, the black paved floor sloped gently down to a large well open to the sky, and beside it a spiral staircase led down to the basement. All

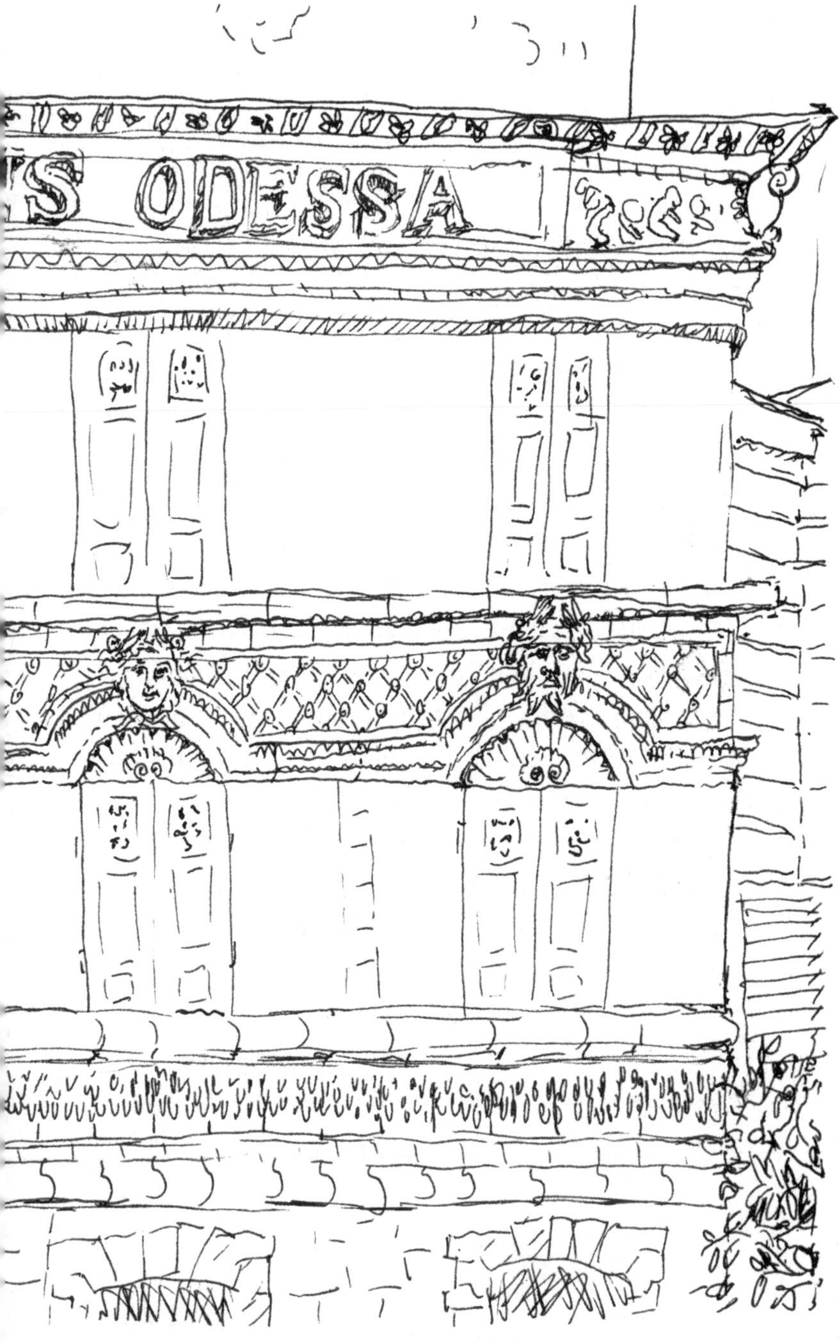
S ODESSA

around it were shops, closed and abandoned, most of them with their metal shutters down. Here again she looked for some trace of the past, but everything obviously dated from the '70s with its smoked glass, concrete, and stainless steel. The three small trees in the middle of the circle, raising their skinny branches toward the gray sky, looked artificial.

Down below, the air was icy, far colder than in the street. A voice behind her startled her, can I help you, miss. It was a very old woman, she was very short and slight with a black hat worn askew, trailing a shopping trolley and carrying a baguette in her hand. When she saw this extremely old, extremely small woman, Hélène realized she'd finally found what she was looking for. She asked the woman if she was from the neighborhood, and did she know what used to be here, repeating her question more loudly to be sure she was heard, yes, where the gallery is there used to be a passage, a narrow street with all sorts of workshops, cabinetmakers, printers, locksmiths, children used to come and play here. Hélène followed the old woman back up the slope, and as she reemerged onto rue d'Odessa, she took a great lungful of air. Standing facing the apartment building, the old lady outlined buildings in the air with her loaf of bread, one on either side of the passage, there was a hosiery store at number 18, and two little businesses at number 16, a photo studio on the left and an upholsterer on the right. Hélène saw them appear magically thanks to that wand of bread, the two shops at number 16 with white lettering on the narrow frontage: STUDIO ASCHER, PHOTOGRAPHY. Did the passage have a name, not an official name, no, but we used to call it Odessa Passage, and the people who lived on rue du Départ called it passage du Départ, Departure Passage. It was all razed to the ground in 1970, along with the station and a good chunk of the neighborhood, so they could build the tower and all the other stuff, imagine the noise, rubble everywhere, like after an air raid, it was a living hell for fifteen years. She couldn't remember the photographer's name, Agère, Ascher, you say, it could have been, the studio had changed hands, she didn't remember the new people, or whether they'd had children. They left during the war, the upholsterer took over the premises to expand his workshop. He repainted the whole shop front brown, it was blue before, dark blue. She didn't know why those people had left, whether they were Jews, no, no idea, she hadn't heard. The upholsterer had left the area after the Liberation. But why do you want to know all this, I'm an archaeology student, I'm interested in old stones, the old woman raised her eyebrows and nodded her head, oh, that's good, that's a very good thing.

On her way back to rue Vavin, Hélène thought about a demolition site she'd once seen in Orléans. The walls of the neighboring building still had expanses of wallpaper, the outlines left by paneling, wardrobes, and fireplaces, and even photos of boats decorating a child's bedroom. There must have been a moment when 16 rue d'Odessa had just been demolished and the already outdated vestiges of Daniel's and his family's life could still be seen, a scrap of wallpaper here, the mark left by a mirror or a painting there.

SHE SLEPT ALONE THAT NIGHT and dreamed of the Odessa Baths. In her dream it didn't look like the place she'd seen, there was a large brick building with strange music emanating from it, like the whistling of an organ with twisted pipes. Dozens of people, mostly children, stood in line, waiting by the door, they were naked and each of them held a piece of soap. Her brother was there, too, much younger than her, they were trying to see what was going on inside, but the windows were frosted, you couldn't see anything. She noticed a familiar face in the crowd, but she couldn't say where she'd seen the girl before.

The dream woke her, and she lay there wide-eyed for a moment with the peculiar lucidity that sometimes comes in the middle of the night. She got up and removed the photo of the earth from the air that was hiding the Soutine painting. It looked different in the half-light, what she now noticed was not so much the suffering of a deformed body as the girl's eyes. Those eyes were too big and were staring right at her.

She ran her hand gently over the portrait as if to soothe the terrified face, and felt a bump in the surface. The frame opened like a door to reveal a small compartment carved into the wall. Inside it was a scroll of yellowed paper with a few words handwritten in Hebrew script:

די גאַנצע וועלט איז איין שטאָט.

PART TWO

December 1999 — April 2000

23

Aboard a Junk on the Yangtze

HÉLÈNE HAD PASSED IT DOZENS OF TIMES, Félicie's Sweet Nothings, a store on rue Bréa that sold all kinds of candy. She went in with Guillaume just before the Christmas break, when they were to be apart for two weeks, he was going to his parents in the south and she to her family in the Auvergne. The tiny shop smelled of caramel; strings of gingerbread Santa Clauses hung under tall glass jars labeled *Ardoise Tiles*, *Vichy Pastilles*, and *Pau Freshwater Pebbles*. Guillaume wanted to buy a few of everything, to taste them, and the saleswoman looked listless and disgruntled as she climbed up the steps to take down the jars one after the other. Hélène had bad memories of hard candy: when she was very little she'd dropped her grandma's candy box, and she could still see the candy all muddled in with pieces of broken porcelain, she could hear her grandfather's deep voice, look at your brother, he's younger than you and better behaved. And her father had said softly, perhaps so that only she would hear, that he too had always been shown his brother as an

77

example, look at Thierry, good as gold, and you're always clowning around.

Guillaume was looking at the old-style metal tins, *Montargis Pralines*, *Nancy Bergamots*, *Cambrai Mint Candy*. The *Nevers Negus* reminded him of one of the *Black Insignia* titles, *The Heirs of the Negus*, it was set in Ethiopia and featured alcohol-soaked colonizers and despicable child-slave traffickers. The saleswoman stopped what she was doing, her hand in midair, did you say something about *The Black Insignia*, and as if she'd taken off a mask, she was now smiling, I know the author, you know, he lives just around the corner. He's my great-uncle, said Hélène. The woman nearly kissed her, Daniel Roche was an old acquaintance, when he'd stopped smoking he'd taken to coming and buying licorice sticks, and they'd got along well, he put dedications in all his books for me, *To my beautiful Félicie*, that's my name, you see. Her cheeks were flushing at this point. She and Guillaume swapped anecdotes from the books, he liked all the colorful characters you came across, she preferred passages full of mystery, her favorite was the latest book, the twenty-third, *Theft in the Fugitives' Garden*. Guillaume wasn't so keen on it, it wasn't really an adventure story, almost a whodunit, he turned to Hélène, it's set in Pompeii, and it's about archaeology, you might like it.

The saleswoman closed up the bags with small red ties, she had a soft spot for the hero, for being so well traveled and absentminded, and for his tattoo, she called him Pete, overfamiliarly. Guillaume couldn't really see what a woman would find attractive about a globe-trotter, never there, always on the far side of the world, she smiled, you wouldn't understand, well, for instance, Daniel's always traveling too, but Lord knows he's had plenty of female admirers, she was slowly putting the parcels into a bag, I mean, take me for example, I can talk about it now, if it had been up to me...

Hélène wondered what she would have looked like twenty years earlier, she was still pretty, with her cute chin and finely drawn eyebrows, but the thought of Daniel having an affair with a woman seemed preposterous, she'd never imagined her great-uncle in love, perhaps because of his childish streak. Félicie was still smiling, her head tilted down toward her calculator, they say sailors have a woman in every port, but Daniel and Pete are the same, their hearts are taken by just one woman and they couldn't ever really love another. Guillaume asked her whom Peter loved, there was no mention of a particular woman anywhere in the books, she smiled and popped an extra packet of biscuits into the bag, they're Wise Word Wafers, have you seen them before, they have things written on them, they're on the house, because you like reading.

Guillaume put the eleven parcels of candy onto the desk in Hélène's bedroom and tasted every one of them, then they lined up the wafers, *What's eating you*, *Can you keep a secret*, *Don't say a word*, and they ate them until there was only one left, *I love you*, which they saved till last.

Late in the evening they went to eat at the Jade Lotus, a little Chinese place farther up rue Vavin. They were the only customers and they chose a table in the small back room. The left-hand wall was decorated with a landscape, steep mountains and women carrying parasols, and this was reflected in a mirror on the right. The radio was playing a monotonous chant sung in a high-pitched voice. This kitsch version of China was all it took for them to travel. They sat side by side practicing their chopstick skills on five-spice duck, giggling when they lost a mouthful. Guillaume told Hélène about the episode in *The Clay Army of Xi'an*, when the young peasant woman finds the first of Emperor Qin's terra-cotta soldiers in a well and realizes with fascination that he has the exact same face as her.

That night the little garret bedroom was a junk drifting over the Yangtze. They slept spooned together, as had become their habit, his arm around her body, soldered to each other, they thought, for all eternity.

14

Grandma Guyon
Unraveling Her Knitting

THE RAILS SPOOLED PAST SLOWLY, crossing over each other and fusing together as the train drew out of Lyon station, a drum rhythm crackled from her neighbor's earphones. Hélène opened up her notes on a lecture, "Byzantine Mosaics, Restoration Techniques," but her own words made her feel tired. Before they were over the river Seine, the boy next to her had fallen asleep. She took *Theft in the Fugitives' Garden* from her bag, the cover showed Peter Ashley-Mill walking through the dead city with Vesuvius smoking in the background, she just wanted to leaf through it.

"Furto stranissimo all'orto dei fuggiaschi." This headline in a local newspaper attracts Peter's attention as he sips his cappuccino beside the Bay of Naples. He is holidaying at the Pensione Miramare because his doctor has told him to get some rest. A strange theft has just taken place in Pompeii, in the garden where dozens of victims were trapped within the glowing cloud. The molds of two bodies have disappeared, a woman and a young child. The article discusses likely collusion, the site is full of people during the day and guarded at night, and these molds are substantial things. Absorbed in his reading, Peter brings the sugar bowl up to his mouth instead of his cup, ponders for a moment, and then gets to his feet. His vacation was not to be a long one.

The police are dragging their feet over the case, Peter explores Pompeii in search of clues, the Baths, the Marketplace, the Villa of the Mysteries. He gets hold of photographs of the stolen molds, the woman lying on her stomach with her arms folded over the face, the child curled up on himself. Why did the thieves choose these particular molds, perhaps they were hoping to retrieve jewelry embedded in the plaster. By blowing up an image from the inquiry, Peter makes out a silhouette in the background. He also uses the old trick with ashes: spread over the floor of the archives room at the Naples Museum of Archaeology one evening, they reveal footprints in the morning.

Hélène suddenly realized that the boy next to her had left, and the train had gone through Nevers, she went back to her reading. In the museum's visitor book Ashley-Mill sees messages in Latin signed *Octavius Quartio*, the name of a man who owned a grand villa in Pompeii before it was demolished by Vesuvius. These messages lead him to the famous volcanologist Jihap Ostrov, who's frequently been heard predicting catastrophes in his strong Russian accent. His neighbors on the island of Ischia where he lives haven't set eyes on him since the theft. Peter manages to get into his house and goes into every room. In one of the bedrooms he finds a peculiarly heavy trunk. He opens the lid.

She was finishing the chapter when the train started to slow down, *Ladies and gentlemen, in a few minutes we will be arriving in Moulins*. Hélène only just had time to get her things together before alighting.

SHE ARRIVED AT HER GRANDMOTHER'S HOUSE at lunchtime, and as soon as the meal was over she went to look for the photo album as usual, but Suzanne said, for heaven's sake, you know those photos by heart. She'd been a widow for only ten months, and Hélène had expected to find her submerged in grief, as she had been back in the summer. But the moment Hélène had stepped into the apartment, she'd noticed Suzanne was almost rejuvenated, wearing a new brightly colored sweater, her eyes brought out by a hint of eye-liner. They were alone together, the rest of the family wouldn't arrive until the next day. Over lunch, Suzanne had talked about how she was keeping busy, still teaching at the hospital, the tai chi, that was new, she'd even done a demonstration in the kitchen, I'm repelling the tiger, I'm shaking up the clouds, stop laughing or I'll fall flat on my face. She had plans, too, she wanted to see a bit of the world, she'd always dreamed of going and listening the whale song in the Gulf of Saint Lawrence, Maurice didn't like travel. Hélène wondered whether the lady was protesting a bit too much in order to convince her, or to convince herself. Could she start a new life at her age, you can start a new game of cards or redecorate the living room, but life itself, can you do that again?

After wiping down the oilcloth, Hélène opened the album on the table. She knew these old family photos well, she and her brother had looked through them every time they spent their vacations in Saint-Ferréol when they were little. At the time, the photos had been strewn pell-mell in a large drawer in a dresser. When Suzanne's mother died, Suzanne had claimed them, Paule didn't put much store by memories of the past. Then Hélène's grandfather had sorted them into big albums, adding headings and dates in his beautiful handwriting.

Hélène thought she remembered the class photo in which Daniel appeared for the first time, she could picture him in an overall and clogs like the other boys. She was wrong. Posing in front of the school's stone façade, captured among some thirty other little lads, Daniel was the only one wearing ankle boots. He was the last child in the middle row, standing slightly apart from the others, you couldn't tell whether he was smiling, he was also the only one whose eyes weren't turned toward the photographer but were looking in a different direction. Perhaps that was why she hadn't recognized him in the Peyrelevades' wedding photo.

The two women pored over the photograph, their heads almost touching, and Hélène could feel Suzanne's breath, with its smell of coffee, on her cheek. Don't you think he looks a bit lost, she asked, who do you mean, Daniel, no he doesn't, why lost. Suzanne pointed at his sweater, its collar peeping out under his overall, I remember that sweater, it was dark red, it was mine before he had it, Grandma Guyon had knitted it up again for him. Suzanne left her finger on the neckline of the overall for a moment, the first time I saw Daniel he was wearing that sweater. As she arrived home that day, she'd found her mother and grandmother pulling the sweater over a child's head. In the end Grandma fetched a pair of scissors to cut the seam, and a stranger's faced popped out. It was only then that Suzanne's mother noticed her, come over, this is the little refugee boy we told you about. She'd pictured a much younger child, one she could mollycoddle, I thought I was going to be able to mother him, no way, he was ten years old and I was twelve, oh, the disappointment, I thought I'd never get used to him, and then in the end.

She'd been jealous at first, like when a baby brother is born and takes your place, how funny, I'd completely forgotten that business with the sweater. Grandma Guyon spent the war years unraveling our knitwear, she'd get Daniel to sit down with his arms in the air so she could wind the hanks of yarn around them, stop scrobbling about, my little goose. She would tell him stories to make him sit still, he always begged for the one about the goat who wants to marry the king's daughter, do you know it, the king insists he provide a palace and a garden, and the goat builds them, but whatever the goat does, the king never keeps his promise.

On the following page, May 1944, Daniel was posing outside the church, with a communicant's armband over his sleeve. He'd been baptized two years earlier, immediately after he arrived, so that he had a certificate. We still used his first name, which didn't sound too Jewish. In the picture he was standing up straight with Paule and Suzanne on one side, and Angèle, their mother, and tiny Grandma Guyon on the other. The sun was making them all squint, giving them a family resemblance, look, his breast pocket's on the right, mommy cut his jacket out of an old one of Daddy's by turning it inside out.

We used to play Happy Families together a lot, could I have Master Block the Butcher's son please, the one with the pig's head in a basket, we still have that game, you know, I should think there are some cards missing now. Daniel always won at hide-and-seek, he'd hide in the attic, under the sink in the back kitchen, in the broom cupboard, in the hayloft, not in the cellar, never, you could walk straight into ours, and he felt that a proper cellar had to be underground. He used to stay hidden until I gave up and stopped looking for him.

Hélène asked whether Daniel talked about Paris, or his family, whether he'd brought any photos or belongings, no, just some clothes in a little suitcase, a few *Bayard* magazines and one tiny little book, but no mementoes. When he talked about his parents, it was just to show off in front of his friends, to big himself up, he used to say his father had a fabulous car, that his aunt in America was a millionaire, yeah right, we all knew that was make-believe. He never said anything about his real life, not even later. All through the war, it didn't matter that the three of us, me, him, and Paule, lived in the same house and slept in the same room even, Daniel was just a sort of temporary brother. A few years after the Liberation, Angèle and Joseph adopted him. When he showed Grandma Guyon his real ID card with the name Daniel Roche on it, she said my goose, my little one, and she cried.

SUZANNE WAS NERVOUSLY FINGERING a corner of the album, June 1950, her marriage to Maurice, the family in the yard, the little cousins standing in front of the bride and groom, their heads hiding her already swollen stomach. She wanted to turn the page, but Hélène held back her hand, people always said they looked alike, particularly in this photo and, hey look, Daniel's not there. Daniel had gone off on his first journey, to the famous aunt in America, who really did exist even if she wasn't a millionaire. Since the end of the war she'd been sending him letters in English, in airmail envelopes, written on paper as thin as the pages of a Bible, he used to reply using a dictionary. In 1950 she paid for his passage by boat, Daddy went all the way to Le Havre with him on the train.

At the end of the album there were a few photos that hadn't been stuck in, including one of Suzanne and Maurice on the beach with their two sons, someone had written *Arcachon, August '59* on the back. Alain was eight and a half, and Thierry seven, but the younger had already caught up with his older brother and would soon overtake him, Alain was still jealous now, at nearly fifty. Hélène adored this photo, the way her grandfather was kneeling on the sand, holding his two boys by the shoulders, their three heads close together, and their mother sitting beside them, watching them. Hélène kept it.

THAT EVENING SHE CAME ACROSS the gray-and-red spine of *The Ferrymen of the Amazon* in the bookcase; it was the only *Black Insignia* title there. It had no dedication, the title page had been torn out. She started reading from where Guillaume had stopped telling her the story, when Peter is getting close to the Indian village, and an arrow whistles past his ear and drives into his backpack. She read on as the hero doubles back through the forest, then slips into the village at night to warn the shaman, Peter is captured and the tribe is attacked by members of the expedition. She became quite caught up by the battle of the Carinaua, led by Zensuna, the cacique's daughter, who was once a friend of the hero's but then withdrew her friendship, in the end she releases him in order to enlist him among her warriors. After that the whites are routed, Peter leaves and crosses the river by canoe while the Indians salute him from the bank, and Zensuna is the last to turn and walk away.

TWO DAYS AFTER CHRISTMAS, when all the family had left, Hélène stayed on in Moulins for a few more hours. Just before saying goodbye to her, Suzanne remembered that Daniel had taken a knife or a bradawl to school one day and had hurt another pupil. The teacher had punished him and confiscated his weapon, and the child had fallen sick as a result of this. Paule probably remembers more about it than me, she has a better memory, and you know what she's like, she always knows everything.

89

15

Daniel's Dagger

HÉLÈNE CAUGHT THE TRAIN TO CLERMONT-FERRAND, fairly
sure that Aunt Paule wouldn't be able to spare any time for
her. Since she'd retired, what with the parish and her various associations, she'd never been so busy, not that being
a midwife was exactly a picnic, as she used to say. When
she was at Saint-Ferréol in the summer, she busied herself in the garden. When Hélène and her brother spent the
Easter vacation and the month of July with their grandparents, Aunt Paule was always there, she was the one who
planned the meals, bandaged up wounds, and predicted
the next day's weather from the color of the sky at sunset.
Whatever the situation, you had to ask Paule, she would
know. Being a widow herself, she'd known which psalm
to read in church at her brother-in-law Maurice's funeral
in February, and she'd supported her devastated sister. She
was dependable, indefatigable, she lived up to the family
name of Roche: she was a rock.

When Hélène arrived at Paule's house, she felt, as she
always did, in the way. The little house was teeming with

volunteers making up parcels to give to the poor on New Year's Day. They took a long time to leave and, because the TV was warning of strong winds, Hélène and Paule closed all the shutters before sitting down to eat. Paule opened a jar of preserved beans and made an omelet, breaking the eggs with one hand, the way Suzanne did. When Hélène had slipped her napkin into its ring at the end of the meal but before she began to clear the table, she finally plucked up the courage to say, do you mind my asking, do you remember when Daniel first arrived. But instead of replying, Paule put a finger to her mouth and strained her ears. A low moan from the living room was growing louder, turning into a roar, a violent booming sound, it was the wind in the chimney and the metal draft stopper rattling demonically.

A moment later the lights went out, Paule fumbled and lit a candle, and the flame guttering in the draft projected shifting shadows behind her. This was far more than the gusts they'd forecast, more than any ordinary storm. Paule turned on an old battery-powered radio, and they sat back down at the table to listen to the news, like during a blackout. A hurricane the likes of which had never been seen, even more violent than the one that had blown across northern Europe the day before, was sweeping over the whole of southern France, here in the Auvergne it wasn't yet at full strength. Sure enough, they could hear it howling more and more loudly, whistling under roof tiles and into pipes, shaking the walls, the whole house creaked, it felt as if the place might collapse. The worst of it was being condemned to listen to this racket without being able to see anything. All along the street around them, shutters smacked like pistol shots, tiles and all sorts of loose items shattered on the ground or against walls, sirens sounded in every direction, it felt like an air raid. Paule wanted to call Suzanne and the rest of the family, but the telephone was cut off and Hélène's cell phone had no signal. At seventy-three, Paule had never seen anything like it. Luckily the houses on her street were a terrace so they would hold each other up. The building Suzanne lived in was solid and modern, she would be in no danger.

It seemed to have reached its paroxysm, the noise was not growing any louder, they could go to bed. Paule gave Hélène a flashlight, and she herself walked up the stairs with the nonchalance of someone who's seen it all before, but the candlestick quivered in her hand. Hélène settled down for the night on the living room sofa, under a picture of Paule's son as a communicant, flanked by photos of Mother Teresa and Sister Emmanuelle, who looked rather less reassuring in the dim light. She thought of Guillaume, he would be safe in the far south, but she'd have liked to call him, just to hear him describe this as some kind of adventure. Zipping up the sleeping bag, she thought how

they'd have clung to each other if they'd been together, like lovers swept away into the torments of hell.

The noise was still too loud for her to sleep so she eventually decided to read *Theft in the Fugitives' Garden* by flashlight. The strangely heavy trunk that Peter finds in Jihap Ostrov's house is actually empty, it is secured to the floor, its false bottom hiding a trapdoor. Lying on beds in the basement, the molds look as if they're sleeping, and Ostrov is just there gazing at them. He's gone half mad and thinks he's Octavius Quartio who left the city the day before the natural disaster, and who searched in vain for his family. Peter grasps that Ostrov also lost his wife and son in an accident. He wants to save these two figures from the next, even more terrifying eruption, which will bury the living along with all memory of the dead.

The wind gradually calmed while she read. Perhaps because she'd been reading through a hurricane, the book left her with something more than its slightly facile detective mystery, an impression of terror. The cover said *for readers 10 years and above.* You'd have to be thoughtless, she felt, or even cruel, to talk about grief and the death of a child and pain that drives people mad to such young readers. She eventually fell asleep. In her dream, the ground at the cemetery in Toulouse was covered in hardened ash and, using her trowel and brush, she exposed a small head. She recognized Jonas's mop of hair. He was so deeply asleep that she couldn't wake him, even when she screamed his name.

In the morning there was still no power in the house, and the radio was announcing dozens of deaths, whole neighborhoods ravaged, forests flattened all over Europe, Paule kept saying, poor people, those poor people. She suddenly jumped to her feet, it must have been even worse in Saint-Ferréol, they had to go and see. Hélène wanted to stop her going, there was no rush, the radio was advising people against making any unnecessary journeys, but Paule never changed her mind, she'd go alone if no one went with her.

Hélène drove Paule's Citroën AX, at least she'd held her ground on that, she had to drive cautiously, slowing down at every corner for fear of finding something blocking the way, driving around fallen branches, sometimes whole trees that the emergency workers had simply pushed to one side. Aunt Paule kept her eyes pinned on the road as if she were driving herself. Hélène made the most of her enforced inactivity, when Daniel was at school in Saint-Ferréol, do you remember him having a knife that the teacher confiscated? Paule turned to look at Hélène, do you think this is the time to talk about that, you'd do better to look where you're going.

At the Issoire exit, the road was partially blocked by a fallen road sign, Hélène slammed on the brakes, the

car stalled, and Paule clutched at her heart. A dagger, I remember, that's what he used to call it, it was a pencil he'd had when he first arrived, he always kept it in his pocket, a normal pencil but sharpened into a really spiky point, he sharpened it on a stone like the knife grinders in Thiers, he said it was very special, its lead was made of black diamond, it was worth a fortune and he could give someone a nasty poke in the eye with it. He scratched Henri Gachon's arm with it one day, what a palaver. The teacher punished Daniel, of course. The next day, maybe it was coincidence, Daniel had a fever, he missed several days of school. Paule heaved a long sigh, our parents had some times with that boy, especially at the beginning, he was so spoiled, before, at home, he must have got away with everything, I don't like cabbage, I don't want this, don't want that. He helped when it suited him, feeding the rabbits, collecting the eggs, he was happy to do that, but he'd pinch his nose and say the chickens stank. We didn't put up with that sort of behavior in our house, Daddy was kindhearted but you couldn't rebel.

The road was climbing up into the mountains, covered in a thin layer of snow; after Chambon-sur-Dolore it became narrower and snaked between the trees, dropping gently back down through Champétières and Susmontargues to Saint-Ferréol-des-Côtes. In places some of the fir trees had been blown over by the storm, and large chaotic clearings now gaped where they had stood. With her hands clamped on her knees, Aunt Paule gazed at the expanses of devastated forest, what a disaster, my God, what a disaster. Before she even stepped out of the car she saw the great oak tree in the courtyard to the house lying broken on the ground, its roots full of earth rearing up toward the sky. She didn't say anything but went straight over to it, put her hand flat against its trunk, and stroked its bark as you would an invalid's forehead. She looked as her mother had at the end, when Hélène used to visit her in her nursing home, and the old girl would mistake her for Suzanne.

They had no electricity here either. Hélène made some tea in the freezing kitchen, and Paule sat down holding her cup in both hands to warm them. Hélène couldn't remember coming to Saint-Ferréol in winter, and for the first time the house, which was empty, closed, and unlit, felt unfamiliar. They went upstairs and opened the shutters in her bedroom, the blue room, and Hélène sat on the bed. Three knots in the joist overhead still made the shape of an elephant's head, and she knew without opening it that in the drawer of the bedside table there was bone cutlery from a child's tea set and an incomplete pack of Happy Families. She thought about the first night Daniel would have spent in this room, with two girls he didn't know, who weren't yet his sisters.

Hélène indicated the bed she was sitting on, when you were little, did you sleep here, yes, with Suzanne, the two of us always slept there. And his little bed was over there, you see, sometimes he talked in his sleep, he would say me too, wait for me, the words didn't mean anything, he'd always forgotten in the morning. She picked up a tuft of wool that had escaped from a seam on the mattress and rolled it around between her fingers. At the end of the war he was too big to sleep with girls, we cleared out the junk room to make a bedroom for him. It was around about then that he went off to boarding school in Clermont, to Lycée Blaise Pascal, the teacher let him take the entrance exam late because of the circumstances, and he caught up afterward. He used to come home to Saint-Ferréol on Saturday evenings.

Hélène opened the door to the attic stairs and climbed up, she didn't remember the ceiling being so low, even in the middle you couldn't stand up straight, a bit of daylight came in through tiny windows at floor level. The little bed had been put away up here, dismantled, she could remember sleeping in it, like every child in the family, and her hand recognized the relief of a sailing ship sculpted into the headboard. It was okay for Daniel, who was small for his age, but he wriggled a lot and was always bumping into the side panels. Their father had replaced these panels with horizontal rails so that he could put out a foot or a leg, you could still see the screw holes. Paule showed her the little wooden shutters Joseph had made to stop the cold air coming through the windows, which had had no glass in them at the time. It was in case Daniel had to hide in the attic, he'd slept there only once, and nothing happened in the end anyway. But he'd liked it in here, so he used to sneak up to read, his teacher would lend him *Treasure Island*, *Robinson Crusoe*, that sort of thing. It was cold in the attic and there was condensation coming out of Paule's mouth as she spoke.

Maurice came over almost every evening at the end of the war, he taught primary school in Saint-Amant-Roche-Savine. He'd set himself the task of finding Daniel's parents in the lists in the papers, it took weeks, months, and then one evening, it was something about the way he rested his bicycle against the wall, we just knew. He went over to Daniel and put his hand on his shoulder, like he probably did with his pupils, but Daniel ducked away and ran up to his bedroom. Maurice spoke in an undertone, he'd seen three names on a list, the father, the mother, and the daughter. Until then we'd thought Daniel was an only child, had he led us to believe that or had we assumed it? Just once, much later, in 1950, he told me, and just me, that she was about the same age as me, well, she would have been. Then nothing more, not even her name. It was right before he set off for Le Havre. Daddy took him up and when he got home he was all in a state, poor Joseph, he told us he'd stayed on the quay watching the ship until it was far, far away, and then he didn't say another thing until the following morning. Hélène pictured her great-grandfather, whom she'd seen only in photographs, an impressive figure of a man with his hand shielding his eyes, watching the liner disappear over the horizon.

When Daniel returned from America, he went to live in Paris, and it was only several years later that he took to coming back to Saint-Ferréol. Paule had taken him in her Citröen to visit their father in the hospital in Ambert a couple of times, and later they'd gone to see their mother in her nursing home. Angèle had forgotten his name, but she would squeeze his hand in hers and say, you know I've still got your medal. It was the Righteous medal that Daniel had ensured they were awarded.

They went back down to the second floor, Hélène closed the shutters up in the blue bedroom. Shortly after the war, the aunt in America, his mother's sister, wanted to adopt him, she was meant to be coming to collect him and had had a letter translated into French, saying she was coming. Our parents didn't say anything, Grandma Guyon shut herself in her bedroom to cry. The aunt could have insisted on having him, there were court cases at the time, she would probably have won. And then they received a second letter, in which she abandoned her claim, without explaining why. Daniel could stay with the

Roches, he could come visit when he was eighteen. No one said anything more about it, but at eighteen, or not even quite that, Daniel set off for New York, if she's still alive now that aunt of his, she must be over ninety. Her name's Mala, I think.

On the way back through the kitchen, Paule opened the cupboard with all the preserved fruits and vegetables, and took a few jars to bring back to Clermont. In the old days, this cupboard didn't have any shelves, we kept brooms in it, one time Daddy shut Daniel in here for God knows what misdemeanor, and he wrote on the wall with his famous pencil that he always kept in his pocket. You could still make out the word SHIT in large letters, and a picture of a dog with its jaws open and a speech bubble saying BEWARE I BITE! They got back into the car, Paule watched Hélène at the wheel, it's amazing how like Suzanne you are, Suzanne at the time of her marriage, twenty, it's very young, when you come to think about it.

HÉLÈNE WENT BACK TO PARIS on one of the first trains to run again, passengers piled in as best they could, sitting on armrests, in corridors, on their bags, a real exodus. Guillaume had stayed down south, so she celebrated the year 2000 with a girlfriend from the Institute of Archaeology. Everyone was waiting for midnight more impatiently than usual, talking loudly, getting excited, and with good reason, they weren't just changing year, but changing century and millennium, it was the eve of a new era. Listening to the old Beatles song "Lucy in the Sky with Diamonds," they messed around blowing smoke rings, the zeros in 2000, then they blew at them to break them up. However much they made fun of millennium scaremongers, of the millennium bug, and the end of the world foretold by astrologers, they still believed in it all a bit, and as the evening wore on and they drank more and more, their laughter became tainted with anxiety. The recent cyclones could have been signs of something; meteorologists had named them Lothar and Martin, like a couple of escaped fairground bears. A very pretty, totally drunk girl stood on the sofa with her hair tumbling loose, invoking the gods and prophesying the end of our civilization, a turning point in the history of the world.

Hélène was slumped on the divan next to a boy who was trying to explain that, mathematically, the third millennium didn't start until January 1, 2001. She'd had too much to drink to follow his reasoning. She was thinking about that aunt in America, that Aunt Mala who might still be alive, it was as if a part of Daniel's family were coming back from the dead. In among the cigarette smoke and the head spin of alcohol, skyscrapers towered before her. In the year 2000, in the spring, she would go to New York.

16

Two Fugitives

ON THE LAST SUNDAY IN FEBRUARY, Daniel invited Hélène to a restaurant as he had promised. She thought he would choose a local brasserie, but he'd told her to meet him on the far side of Paris, at the Petit Navire in Saint-Ouen. While in the area he wanted to show her around the flea market which, he claimed, was worth a quick visit. The manageress at the restaurant called him Monsieur Ascher, he introduced Hélène, my great-niece, so you're a great-uncle already, oh yes, I was only born yesterday but it's been a long day.

He'd recently returned from his travels, Hélène was expecting him to talk about Mauritania and the desert, and for him to go rummaging through a pocket in his parka on the coatrack to produce, say, a desert rose, but no. She was the one who ended up telling him about her trip to the Auvergne, the terrifying storm, her perilous expedition, driving from one obstacle to the next, the big old uprooted oak, she laid it on a bit thick, and he listened, wide-eyed and entertained. Paule told me stuff about you, Uncle Dan-

104

iel, when you were little, ouch, God knows what that Paulette told you, the Parisian, the spoiled child, I guess. He looked down at his plate and toyed with his knife. She also mentioned your aunt in New York, ah yes, my aunt Mala.

Mala had managed to get out of Poland from Danzig just before the war, and she reached America with her husband and son. Afterward, along with so many people who went to such lengths to piece their families together again, she'd traced Daniel to Saint-Ferréol and had even taken steps toward adopting him. But the same boy who dreamed of America so ardently through the war years was now frightened by the thought, leaving forever, do you see, I realized I'd become a little Roche, a little kid from the Auvergne, I'd got the accent. He ran his finger around the edge of his plate as if around the shores of a distant island. And then Mala abandoned the quest, she didn't come to claim him, she just made him promise that when he was eighteen he would come to see her, maybe she felt it was better for me, and she didn't speak French, it would have been a difficult process for her.

And so in 1950 he kept his promise and made the crossing. It was the year of his school graduation exams, the "bachot" they used to call it then, but he left in April without even taking the tests. Why didn't he wait until the summer vacation, let's just say I wanted to see a bit of the world, he shrugged, I'd got to that stage, young and fancy-free, you know, he added with a laugh, and anyway who said globe-trotters were ever sensible.

Mala was a beautiful woman, always well turned out and manicured, she was a hairdresser and she had a callus on her finger from the scissors. She and her husband had welcomed him like a son, they wanted to show him the best of America, Uncle Jacob wasn't the talkative sort but he wore his heart on his sleeve, cousin Sammy took him to see everything, Brooklyn and all that, in fact their neighborhood was called Little Odessa. He and his cousin used to earn a bit of pocket money washing hair and sweeping up in the salon, it was weird, those piles of different-colored hair all mixed together. They'd hoped Daniel wouldn't leave, but he was homesick and after three months he went back to France.

Hélène asked whether his aunt was still with us, he coughed, sadly not, he picked up his glass and looked at his red wine in the light, well, could you really call that being with us. Uncle Jacob's dead, and she, well, she's lost her mind, she can't walk, nothing works anymore, at ninety-six it's understandable. But he still saw Sammy, who came to Paris from time to time. He drained his glass.

New York, yes, she wanted to go there with Guillaume for the Easter vacation. He didn't know America either, they could spend a week in a cute hotel. Daniel said why not, why not, but he was shaking his head at the same time,

I'd really like to go see your cousin and your aunt in New York. He put his glass down a bit too quickly and the dregs of his wine splashed onto the tablecloth. Sam, of course, he'd let him know, he'd give Hélène his phone number, Sam had done well, he was a dentist, very kind, so was his wife, he had two daughters from two different marriages, but my aunt, what's the point, she's a sorry sight, she won't have a clue who you are, she doesn't recognize her own son now, Hélène, whatever you do don't go to see her. Hélène nodded but the more Daniel protested, the more convinced she was that she absolutely had to see this Aunt Mala before it was too late.

THEY SPENT THE AFTERNOON wandering through the flea market, a whole world in itself, Daniel knew every last little alleyway, look, that's Ali Baba's cave, you can find anything and everything in there, crystal door handles, tap shoes, and even Beethoven's actual ear trumpet, you just have to look. At the Vernaison market on rue des Rosiers, he showed her a tiny shop where they sold butterflies in glass cases, feathers, birds' eggs, and semiprecious stones from all over the world. Lots of the traders greeted him as he went by, calling him Monsieur Ascher or even Daniel.

They drifted along, stopping to leaf through a book, a collection of postcards, or a stamp album, to open up a board game or study an engraving. Sometimes he would find something interesting, sometimes she would, they saw each other reduced to miniatures through the wrong end of a telescope, they turned the handle on a toy-sized carousel, tried on an opera hat, an English World War II helmet, it turned out she hadn't wasted her day. He insisted on giving her a large magnifying glass with a horn handle, it might be useful on her archaeological digs.

Here, Daniel didn't have the hurried Charlie Chaplin walk he had in his own neighborhood in Montparnasse, where he always seemed to be playing a part, laughing too enthusiastically, speaking too loudly, walking too quickly. It was as if he'd slowed the film, established the right rhythm. Along these cluttered streets, he adjusted to his own age, an old man surrounded by old things.

He was keen to introduce Hélène to his great friend Elie Frailich, whose shop was at the far end of one alley. It was like a minimuseum of the history of photography, with display cases full of cameras, flashes, tripods, and electric eyes. Elie was sitting in his shop reading the paper, he was expecting them, hi there, Dani, hi, my old brother. He was a short, thickset man, a jovial character who hugged Daniel then looked at him affectionately. Next he turned to Hélène, Dani's told me so much about you, I'm Elie Frailich, Dani's first friend, no doubt about that, I've known him since he was born, and that's saying something. They sat around a small table as if the shop were a living room, and the people strolling around the flea market only yards away from them simply didn't exist. Elie had some coffee in a thermos and some poppy seed biscuits made by his wife, eat, Hélène, go on, eat.

The two friends had a distinctive way of talking one after the other and at the same time so that neither voice smothered the other, it was like a dialogue on stage. Elie remembered how they'd met when they were tiny, Daniel picked up the story, at the time of his birth his father worked in the Frailich Studios in the Belleville district of Paris, before setting up his own place on rue d'Odessa. Elie loved Isaac Ascher's jokes, did you take a shower, no why, there's one missing. He was five years older than Dani and clearly remembered the first time he saw him, at two weeks old, you were so *mies*, thank you my old brother, I tell you, Hélène, *mies* means ugly in Yiddish, they laughed, slapped each other on the shoulder, then Daniel relaxed back into his chair.

Elie picked up his Sunday paper from behind Daniel, have you seen, this little Cuban survivor, they found him out on the ocean, tied to a life preserver, his name's Elián, nearly my name, he should really be called Moses, saved from the waters. Moses is my second name, said Daniel, and Elie actually saved my life. No I didn't, Elie replied,

109

we saved each other, it was the great escape, but you must know this story, Hélène.

They told her how they'd escaped from a children's home they were in, it was run by UGIF, the Jewish organization, you know, on rue Lamarck, that was in '42, in late July. Elie was fifteen, Daniel ten, and they'd ended up in a group of Jewish children who'd been separated from their families and put into care there, it was so boring in that home, the food was terrible, and Elie particularly loathed being locked up and at the mercy of police raids. He was right, Daniel went on, those places were traps, the kids who stayed there were rounded up. The two boys had made the most of an outing to run away, hiding in a lean-to down at the bottom of a yard until people stopped looking for them. While they were hiding, they'd unpicked the yellow stars on their jackets with Elie's penknife, what had their mothers been thinking sewing them on with such tiny stitches. Obviously, they had to leave all their things in the home, except what they were wearing and one or two treasures in their pockets.

Elie had taken Daniel all the way to the Luxembourg Gardens, he knew where he was going from there. You know, Hélène, my brother Elie was heroic, a real mensch, it would have been easier for him to run away without me, and on top of everything else, I was so frightened, now that's true, said Elie, I can confirm that, you were scared to death. Still, you were cleverer than me, they didn't find you. Why clever, I was just lucky, I met Colette Peyrelevade on rue Vavin, she was just coming out of number 4, she was young and pretty, and I was ashamed of myself, they'd shaved off my hair at the home because of nits, and I wanted to cross the street, but she soon caught up with me and she took me into the building with her. I stayed in hiding with the Peyrelevades until they found someone who could take me to a safe place, as they called it. I spent three weeks reading, they lent me storybooks and a whole adventure series, you knew those ones too, Elie, do you remember, with Prince Eric and the scouts, the mysterious numbers on his gilded silver bracelet, and a camp called Birkenwald. Yes of course, of course I remember.

DANIEL ESCORTED HÉLÈNE BACK TO THE METRO and then headed off in a different direction. A little way along the line, Hélène realized she'd left the vintage magnifying glass in Elie's shop. She took the train back in the other direction, and successfully found the Marché Vernaison, but she got lost in the maze of alleyways and when she finally reached Elie's shop, it was almost dark and most of the stores had lowered their metal shutters. Elie's was only half closed, and there was a light on inside. She bent down and saw him sitting at the table under a bright light, with some contraption he'd started dismantling, she startled him when she gave a couple of little knocks on the metal shutter, oh, it's you again. They looked everywhere but didn't find the magnifying glass.

Elie showed her what he was repairing, it was an enlarger, a Leitz, a marvel of optical precision, beautiful, isn't it, he stroked the black metal bulb shape. Hélène took her wallet from her purse, he smiled, I wasn't saying that to make you buy it. She took out the small piece of paper she'd found behind the picture in her bedroom, she hadn't shown it to anyone yet, she hadn't dared, do you know any Hebrew, of course, let's have a look. He opened it out and started to laugh, it's not Hebrew, it's Yiddish, *Di gantse velt iz eyn shtot*, the whole world is one town, it's a proverb, the world's a village, it's a small world, where did this phylactery come from.

Hélène put it back in her wallet, you said this was a Leitz, yes, my father had the same one, and Isaac Ascher did, too. Dani loved watching his father developing photographs, their darkroom was downstairs from their apartment, behind the shop, you got to it through a trapdoor. The red light, the way faces appeared in the developer, it fascinated him. I hated all that, my father used to make me hang up the rinsed prints on a line, the water ran down my sleeves, he smoothed his hand over his left arm, and his sleeve bunched up slightly, revealing something that looked like a bruise. And now, it's funny, I'm the one living with all this stuff, and Dani doesn't have any of it, not even the simplest little camera. It's a shame, she said, with the all the traveling he does. No, I think it's because of the roundup, because he was in the darkroom that day, you knew that. No, you didn't know. That morning, it was in '42, July 16th, a neighbor had tipped them off and Isaac just had time to go down to the darkroom before the police arrived. Everyone thought they were only taking the men, not women and children, so there was no need for Dani to hide, but maybe because he loved the darkroom so much, he went down with his father and, because it all had to happen in a hurry, his mother closed the trapdoor.

They crouch down there in the dark, the father holding Dani in his arms as if to stop him getting away, they hear knocking on the door, footsteps, men's voices, not loud enough to make out what they're saying, and then suddenly his sister's voice, talking loudly, practically screaming, if you take my mother I'm going, too. The father lets go of his son, gets up, but then no, he sits back down and takes the child again, Dani can feel Isaac's heart hammering against his back, he squeezes the boy harder and harder, puts his hand over his mouth, it's the first time in his life his father has hurt him. As he talked, Elie stooped over and reassembled the enlarger in the light from his lamp, his salt-and-pepper hair almost luminescent in the glow.

They stay like that for a long time, a very long time. In the end his father lets go, Dani starts crying, why did you hurt me, Isaac opens the trapdoor, which isn't easy because the mother and sister had dragged boxes over it to hide it, and they go up to the apartment. Daddy, why, why did you hurt me. His father's like a statue, he doesn't answer, he says listen, just that one word, listen, and Dani stops pleading and suddenly he hears it, too. Silence. No one left. His sister was seventeen years old, she was French. They weren't taking French Jews that day. Weren't meant to be. On her papers it said Annette Ascher, we called her Hana.

Isaac took Daniel to the children's home that same day, then he intended to go to the police station to say there'd been a mistake, he promised Dani he'd come back for him the next day, but Daddy, if you're coming back tomorrow, why are you blessing me. And it was there, in that children's home on rue Lamarck, that Daniel and I met up again. The kids were talking about all sorts things, what they'd seen, what they'd heard said. Dani was one of the most talkative. But he didn't tell me the story of the darkroom until years later, he told the children in the home that he'd secured a rope across the doorway to trip the policemen, that he'd blinded them with feathers by disemboweling a pillow, that he'd knocked over a pile of cardboard boxes in the corridor to slow them down, that thanks to him his whole family had had time to jump out the window and escape along passage du Départ, great name for it, Departures Passage, that they'd caught a ship to America and he'd soon be joining them. Elie had finished putting the enlarger back together and was polishing it with a soft cloth.

Either way, once we'd run away from the home, he came out of things better than me, Dani did, they didn't catch him again. I did my bit for the Resistance, took some risks. In all my bad luck, I did have one stroke of luck, I looked older than I was. And that's what saved me back there. I wouldn't say I saw death up close in Birkenau. I was inside it, you see, he pulled up his left sleeve, revealing his tattooed forearm. I was right inside death.

He put the enlarger back in its display cabinet and locked it up. On top of the cabinet, Hélène noticed the plastic bag containing the vintage magnifying glass with the horn handle.

17

Dinner with Uncle Sam

Guillaume slept through most of the flight, lulled by the thrum of the plane, his head lolling sometimes toward the window, sometimes toward Hélène. She woke him when the plane started its descent, as the rising sun sliced almost horizontally onto Manhattan's skyscrapers. A funny location for archaeologists, this brand-new vertical city with hardly any history. For the first two days they did a lot of walking around New York, delighted to discover that the design of the paving slabs on the sidewalks matched the layout of the city. They recognized images seen in the movies, a woman with ten dogs on leashes in Central Park, a businessman handcuffed to his briefcase on Wall Street; they bought a pencil from a blind man who had a sign around his neck, please buy a pencil, Guillaume thought he was just like the philosopher-beggar that Ashley-Mill comes across in *Meet Me in Soweto*.

On the second evening she called Sam Seligman, and he suggested they come by his office toward the end of afternoon the next day. The huge waiting room with its marble floor and leather chairs was empty at that time of day, and Sam appeared in a blue tunic, smiling at them with his perfect teeth. He was very sorry, a patient had just arrived as an emergency and he wouldn't be able to see them. He didn't look much like his cousin Daniel, he was taller and far more muscular, but his hair, which was probably dyed, had the same wave over his forehead. He invited them to dinner at his apartment in two days' time, his secretary would give them the address. Hélène was disappointed, she'd been expecting a warmer welcome, she read the card on the way back down in the elevator, *Your next appointment is*, here the secretary had written the address and the date, *Thursday, April 20, 7 pm*, Hélène felt about as little enthusiasm as she would have for a dental appointment.

She hadn't grasped that Sam Seligman was inviting them to a special dinner, he'd said Passover, but she didn't recognize this English word for what it was. There to welcome them were Sam, his wife Libby, who was much younger than him, their teenage daughter, and Sam's other daughter from his first marriage. They were all dressed up for the evening, Sam was in a suit and tie, and, in taking off his blue tunic, he had also lost his professional reserve. Guillaume was very soon asking, may I call you Uncle Sam, which made him laugh out loud, and the two of them headed off toward the dining room.

117

By the time Hélène joined them, Guillaume was wearing a white satin *kippah*. Libby asked her daughter to let Bubbe know everyone was here, and Hélène imagined she was referring to a young man. The teenage girl came back after a few minutes and she held the door open while a home nurse steered in a wheelchair, in it was an elderly lady with carefully curled white hair and wearing an indigo blue jacket, her red lips and highly rouged cheeks made her look like an old photograph that had been touched up with color. Hélène didn't realize straightaway that this was Aunt Mala. She'd pictured her in faded colors, swathed in grief, like a relic from a bygone age, and only her eyes were close to what she'd imagined, an even paler blue than Daniel's, as if they'd been washed out.

Mala looked at Guillaume and Hélène for a long time, one after the other, even after Sam had done the introductions, my mother, we call her Bubbe which means grandma in Yiddish, and Julia who's from the Philippines and who looks after her. Julia pushed Mrs. Seligman's wheelchair up to the table and sat to her right, the old lady didn't take her eyes off Hélène. Daniel had said whatever you do don't go and see her, she won't have a clue who you are, and yet she seemed to know exactly who Hélène was.

Sam was at the far end of the table, officiating as the patriarch with a Haggadah, a silver pitcher and a round dish of peculiar foodstuffs. Hélène watched Sam's younger daughter take the pitcher and pour some water over her father's hands, she felt cut off from home by more than an ocean. She'd associated Hebrew rituals with a world of age-old stones that were buried or had been lost, but here was an American teenager with braces on her teeth quite naturally reenacting these ancestral gestures.

As the youngest person there, the teenager had been given the responsibility of asking the ritual question, why is this night different from all other nights, and her father replied by reading out an account of the exile from Egypt, the plague of Egypt, and the crossing of the Red Sea. Hélène gradually shook off the uncomfortable feeling that she had gate-crashed a family celebration to which she didn't belong. Sam listed the gifts of the Lord, and after each one the gathering had to chant *Dayenu*, that would have been enough. Hélène murmured the word at first, afraid of feeling ridiculous, but her voice slowly grew stronger and mingled with the others, Julia chanted the loudest, as if to lend half her voice to Mrs. Seligman. The old woman nodded her head in time, her eyes pinned on her son and a dazzling smile on her face.

THEY SHARED ROOTS, bitter herbs, salty water like tears, and still other foods that recalled the suffering of the

Hebrew slaves during their flight from Egypt. After every prayer they all said *Amen*, and Hélène felt she was back among more familiar liturgies.

Sam raised his glass, and suddenly his tone of voice changed; from the way all heads turned toward him, Hélène could tell he'd broken with the immutable ritual. He spoke of his cousin Daniel who hadn't been back to New York since 1950, I would so love him to be here with us tonight. Hélène pictured Daniel sitting among them, to Libby's right perhaps, his hair awry and his collar askew. She could now see the similarities between the two cousins. When Sam wasn't smiling, his lips were just like Daniel's, the upper one thin and almost straight, and the lower one fuller, more like a child's. She looked at Mala but couldn't see whether her mouth was the same too under all that lipstick that was gradually rubbing off as Julia fed her spoonfuls of broth and wiped her mouth with a napkin. Julia whispered something in the old lady's ear, she opened her eyes, then nodded very slowly. Sam was still talking, Dan and I could have grown up together, like brothers, my parents would have been his parents, we could all have been so happy, but it didn't work out like that. No one, apart from Hélène, seemed to notice that the old lady had grabbed Julia's wrist and was squeezing it astonishingly hard. She sat like that, frozen, eyes closed, for some time.

When Hélène and Guillaume were leaving, Julia tugged at Hélène's arm, come over at two o'clock tomorrow, apartment 412, on the same floor, come on your own. Hélène wondered whether Julia herself had taken the initiative to invite her, or whether Mala had instructed her to with some hidden sign.

18

Mala's Secret Card

MALA SELIGMAN WAS SITTING at the far end of the living room, near the window, her hair was less neatly arranged than the day before and her tired face looked more vulnerable. She straightened herself up slightly when she heard Hélène come in, and she looked at her for some time without smiling, studying her face, then scrutinizing her as a whole, right down to her feet. She turned to look outside for a moment, and then back at Hélène, and she nodded gently, to indicate that she recognized her and was perhaps inviting her to sit down.

Julia gestured toward the sofa opposite the old lady and served three cups of very weak American coffee, which Hélène rather liked. Mala had thin, very white hands with bright red nails, and she kept them crossed. The callus Daniel had mentioned was clearly visible on one of her fingers. There was a pile of photo albums beside her, Julia explained that they'd spent hours looking through them together, discovering details that no one had so far noticed, a train in the distance, the striped fabric of a garment, a chimney on a roof. Hélène was surprised to hear Julia talking about it in front of the old woman, but Mala nodded slowly in agreement and then pointed to the bottom of the pile. Julia pulled out an album that was more worn than the others and came over to sit near Hélène, they were old photos, and she told the story as if it were her own. The little town was called Kamiensk, look, there, that's Mrs. Seligman's father's house, he was a watchmaker. This is her with her sister, they were born the same year, Rywka in January and Mala in December, people thought they were twins, their own parents got them mixed up sometimes, they had fun passing themselves off as each other. Their mother always had the same dresses made for them, you can't see in the picture but these ones here were pink, the fabric was bought in the market in Manila, I'm sorry, I mean Radomsko. Julia started laughing, I'm confusing things with my own memories. Other people only noticed how alike they were, but they themselves were interested in their differences, Rywka was slightly taller, half an inch or so, and Mala had a beauty spot under her left eye. This is Rywka with her husband and little Hana, just before they left for France. And this is Mrs. Seligman's parents, it's the last picture of them that was sent to her, her father the watchmaker was always photographed with a watch in his hand, her mother is sitting up nice and straight, and smiling, so that her children who are now so far away don't worry. This is little Sammy in Central Park, pointing at an airplane, wasn't he cute, old Mala in her wheelchair agreed with a tilt of her head.

Julia carried on turning over the pages, Rywka's husband was a photographer, she sent a lot of pictures from Paris. They featured Daniel, almost always sitting on someone's knee, held in someone's arms, being kissed, he was a lovely-looking child, with his lock of hair over his forehead, sometimes smoothed sleekly to one side, sometimes tousled, perhaps that was what Aunt Paule had meant by a spoiled child. The last photo showed all four of them, on Daniel's tenth birthday, June 2, 1942, it was written in the margin, he was holding a book so small that his hand almost completely obscured its cover. Julia lowered her voice, the father, mother, and daughter were murdered by the Germans, she turned the page swiftly, the old lady was looking out the window again.

They ate very crumbly biscuits made without flour or yeast, for Passover, Julia explained. Mala reached a hand toward the sideboard, and Julia took something from behind a stack of plates, an old red-and-white can labeled *Carnation Powdered Milk*, she opened it but Mala couldn't get her gnarled hands inside it. Julia took out a fob watch in tarnished silver, it was the one her father had given her as a wedding present, the hands were forever frozen on ten past twelve, it could have been midday or midnight. He'd given the same model to each of his children, Lord alone knew where the others were. Julia took a newspaper cutting from the can, a half page of the *New Jersey Herald* from July 16, 1962, with a picture of a group of children taking part in a soap bubble contest, giant bubbles drifted away above their heads. A ring of blue ink circled a woman standing alone on a balcony in the background, leaning down so you couldn't see her eyes, Mala pointed to her and produced a sort of rolled *r* sound, Rywka, Julia asked, she nodded yes, but Rywka had been dead a long time by 1962, and Mala shrugged her shoulders as if to say go figure. And it had to be said that the woman on her balcony did look like Rywka, a Rywka who hadn't aged. Julia took one of the old woman's hands in her own slender hands and held it for a long time, Mala looked exhausted, she closed her eyes and seemed to go to sleep.

Almost immediately Julia delved deep into the can and peeled something from the side. It was an airmail envelope addressed to Mr. Daniel Ascher, it had been there for years. The day Julia had suggested mailing it, Mala, who could still talk at the time, had threatened to throw her out. The envelope had never been sealed, inside it was a second, yellowed envelope containing a card that Julia handed to Hélène. On its back was a postage stamp featuring Marshal Pétain and stamped by the *Office of*

Censorship, there were also two addresses, on the left *Madame R. Ascher, Drancy Camp*, and on the right, *Madame Le Guillou, 16 rue d'Odessa, Paris* XIV. On the front were a few lines of sloping handwriting with large assertive letters, I guess they had to write in French, Julia said, but I understand most of it.

July 27, 1942

Dear Madame Le Guillou, My mother and I are in Drancy, we will soon be leaving for an undisclosed destination. We know that my father has also been arrested, but he isn't with us. My mother would very much like you to forward this card to her sister: Mrs. Seligman, 3139 Coney Island Avenue — Brooklyn — New York — United States. Dear lady, we would like to thank you from the bottom of our hearts for helping us. We will write again as soon as we can. Annette Ascher. Below, in different writing with poorly joined-up letters and several crossings-out, were three lines in which every word appeared to have been spelled out, *Mala, my sister, take care of Daniel as if he were your own son. I entrust him to you. Don't forget us. Your Rywka.*

On the yellowed envelope, above the New York address copied out by the neighbor, the postmark indicated September 9, 1945. Madame Le Guillou could have sent the card immediately after the Liberation, but she'd kept it languishing in the bottom of a drawer. Was she the neighbor who'd warned the Aschers before the roundup, or the wife of the upholsterer who took over the shop and the apartment, one and the same perhaps?

A sudden clattering of crockery made them jump, Julia ran to hold back Mala's arm before she smacked her cup against the table again. The old woman was surprisingly strong, Julia could hardly restrain her one hand while she parried the blows that Mala was aiming at her with the other. Come on, Julia tried to laugh about it, she gets like this every now and then, she even hurts herself on purpose sometimes, stop that please, I'll put everything away if you let go of that cup. The old woman let go of the broken handle she was still holding, she was breathless, eyeing Julia furiously as the latter put the card and the envelopes back into the can and shut it all away in the sideboard. When Mala had the key in her hand, which was bleeding slightly, she finally slumped deep into her wheelchair, and she sat there inertly, staring at the blank screen of the television. Below her reddened eyelids, her irises looked an even paler blue. She didn't so much as turn her head when Hélène came over to say goodbye, close enough to notice, under her left eye, a beauty spot that made a sort of tear shape.

19
The Doldrums

SAM TOOK HÉLÈNE AND GUILLAUME TO THE AIRPORT two days later, it was a Sunday, early in the morning, Hélène sat in the back of the Range Rover and she could see Sam's eyes in the rearview mirror. He was talking about Daniel again, we spent the war like the two halves of the afikomen, the broken Passover matzo, half of which is hidden and then later reunited. When they saw each other for the first time in 1950, it was like a reunion, Dan was the brother he wished he'd had, Sam confided in him and in the evenings they went out together with friends. Sam introduced him to girls, pretty Jewish girls from Little Odessa, but Dan was shy, or perhaps he'd left a sweetheart in France, although he never mentioned one.

When it came to drinking, though, he didn't hold back, he'd end the evening totally drunk every time, and when he was drunk he said and did the funniest things. One time he started singing at the top of his lungs in the middle of a street, another he insulted a bartender who wouldn't serve him because he was underage, and still another time it took three of them to stop him throwing himself into the bay, shrieking that he was going to get himself arrested. Sam laughed as he related these memories, Hélène could see his eyes in the rearview mirror. I remember another night, it was his birthday, June 2nd, we had to carry him all the way home, that was the day I realized he was homesick and he was prepared to invent whatever it took to go back to France. He kept saying, let me go, I have to get back there, she's expecting a baby and I'm the father, I'm eighteen, I can marry her now. I quieted him down and put him to bed, but he kept on going, they drove me out, I'm an ungrateful good-for-nothing, a bad son, they sent me to New York, I must go home. He was crying like a little kid, I was worried he'd wake my parents, I did my best to console him, stop ranting, Dan, you came to New York because it was planned a long time ago, you know that, you promised my mother. Then the next day, as usual, he didn't remember any of it, it was really funny. Sam tried to make eye contact with Hélène in the rearview mirror, perhaps to see whether she was laughing too, and his eyes froze. From the Brooklyn Bridge he showed them the city silhouetted behind them, look at that, the New York skyline, that's America for you, when you come back they'll have built new skyscrapers, even taller ones, everything's possible here.

HÉLÈNE WANTED TO SLEEP ON THE PLANE, but the things Sam had told them lingered in her mind. Of course you could see it as the fabrications of a teenager on vacation, a drunken evening and a few empty words, an excuse to go back to France, but it might be more than that. And what if Daniel's ranting wasn't fabrication, what if the drink had simply loosened his tongue, and this business of fathering a baby were true? The woman expecting his child might have been from Clermont, Daniel had been a boarder at the lycée in those days, he must have gone out from time to time, or perhaps a girl from Saint-Ferréol.

He'd promised his aunt he would go see her when he was eighteen. Yet he didn't wait until his birthday, he left in April, before his school exams. Maybe that was because of this business with a pregnancy. He hadn't gone to run away but because he'd been forced, because he'd been driven out of Saint-Ferréol, and out of the Roche family. If Joseph, her great-grandfather, took him all the way to the liner, and waited until it left the quay and dwindled on the horizon, then it was to be sure that Daniel didn't get back off the thing. He had to go into exile, disappear, be forgotten. Abandon his child. He was almost a child himself. He could at least have waited until his sister's marriage to Maurice in June. Hélène remembered that Suzanne was four months pregnant at the time. Pregnant with Alain, her father.

The plane banked around toward the dark blue ocean so suddenly that some passengers screamed at the dizzying sensation, and Guillaume jolted in his sleep. Hélène didn't react.

She was thinking about that photo taken on the beach at Arcachon, the one she'd brought home with her from her grandmother's house. It showed Maurice hugging his two sons, Alain and Thierry, in equal measure. The love between the father and his eldest son was clearly there, running along that man's arm held around that little boy's shoulders. That love was visible, palpable, in both directions.

Suzanne was also in the photo, sitting next to them. She was turned not toward the photographer but toward her husband and the two boys, looking at them tenderly but also with a hint of anxiety, as if the balance between the father's arms was a fragile one, as if it wouldn't have taken much to upset that balance. But perhaps Hélène was interpreting it like that, a mother's loving gaze is always a little anxious. That didn't mean anything.

There was still her grandfather's hostility toward Daniel, the foul moods that always gripped him when Daniel was around, so systematically that no one even noticed. It wasn't hate, but they couldn't be in the same room together, everything about his brother-in-law exasperated Maurice, his childishness, his showmanship, his loony appearance, as Maurice called it. But that didn't mean anything either.

Hélène tried to remember details, words and gestures, the few memories of her father's childhood she'd been told about. The very day he was born, Suzanne would say, laughing, it was November 3, and Maurice came to the hospital with a bunch of chrysanthemums, poor man, he knew nothing about the language of flowers. There were awkward things said about Alain, he'd become a difficult child, he was compared to his better-behaved, more biddable younger brother who was already taller than him by the time he was eight. People often said that Thierry was the image of his father, with his height and build, and that Alain was like his mother with his almond-shaped eyes, but that's not what a boy wants to hear. Anyway, thought Hélène, family likenesses don't mean anything either, your father is the man who gets up in the night when you're frightened, who finds the lost piece of jigsaw puzzle, who tells you off when you're naughty. The one who's there. Alain's father was Maurice.

Still, Daniel had always shown a preference for Alain, an indulgence he didn't show Thierry. Hélène thought of all the presents he'd given her parents, and still gave them, for the house, for her studies and for her brother's.

Maurice was definitely her grandfather, though. How could her parents and grandparents have lied to her all these years, when they'd always taught her to tell the truth? She'd rather not know, she'd prefer never to ask

Suzanne this unthinkable question, is Maurice really your son's father, nor ask Daniel either, and her father even less. And waiting until one or another of them confessed, on their deathbed, in a cracked voice, like in the movies, that was ridiculous.

Her grandfather was definitely Maurice Chambon. Her ancestors were Chambons and Roches, Auvergne stock whose names and dates were known, the places where they were born and where they died, she'd seen their houses and their tombs in the cemetery. She wasn't about to replace them with ancestors she knew nothing about, uprooted people scattered goodness knew where in the world, a family of ghosts, a nomadic tribe, glimpsed through the fog, on the far bank of a river. They were nothing to do with her. Otherwise nothing would mean anything anymore. Who would her father's grandparents be, and what about her, where would she be from? No, her name was Hélène Chambon. Not Hélène Ascher.

The plane rose above the clouds, the ocean disappeared. Perhaps that was what becoming an adult was, emerging from the clouds, leaving behind the sweet half-light of childhood, coming out into the blinding clarity of a truth you haven't asked to know. And now for the first time, this girl who'd never been afraid of heights was aware of all thirty thousand feet of emptiness beneath her.

PART THREE

April–July 2000

20

The Horn-Handled Magnifying Glass

DANIEL WAS NOT AT HOME when Hélène returned from New York, he was traveling again. It was surprising that he'd left without warning her, without even leaving a note, when back in December he'd let her know he was going to Mauritania. The caretaker hadn't seen him in the last few days, usually when he went away, he came past with his suitcase to say goodbye and ask her to keep his mail, but not this time. Perhaps the Peyrelevades would know, Hélène said, no, Mrs. Almeida couldn't think why he would have told them rather than her. Hélène knew there was no reason at all to worry about Daniel, he was a grown-up, he didn't have to explain himself. And anyway, as when she first came to Paris in September, she didn't really mind him being away, quite the opposite, she was apprehensive about seeing him again.

Luckily, she had a deadline to hand an essay in at the institute, and she was completely absorbed in writing it. She had chosen as her subject the mosaic at Germigny-des-Prés, which she'd known since her childhood. Her father had first shown it to her, he liked the little Roman-esque oratory, a curved white building like churches in the south, transported by mistake to the middle of a village on the banks of the Loire, and they'd spent many minutes side by side gazing up at the mosaic in the semicircular vault, with him crouching to be level with her and pointing at various details. As a very young girl she'd fallen in love with the two perfectly androgynous archangels whose vast wings brushed together tenderly.

She took out some photos she'd taken at Germigny and taped them to the walls of her room, in front of her desk and around the bed. She was living inside the mosaic, inhabiting it, she knew every detail of it by heart, the empty Ark of the Covenant, the flitting cherubim in the center, the Savior's hand marked with a stigma, emerging from a dark rainbow. In fact she could have drawn them with her eyes closed. The symmetrical archangels were as alike as twins, but if you looked more closely, there were four marks forming the shape of a cross on the halo of the one to the left, he was the Christian archangel, and the other, with the plain halo, was the Jewish archangel. And this reminded her of Daniel. The Ark of the Cov-enant, which is thought to have housed the stone tablets on which the Ten Commandments were written, reminded her of Moses, Elie Frailich, his story of escape, and Dan-iel again. She dreamed of that mosaic almost every night, she saw herself picking up tessellated tiles that had fallen onto the floor of the apse, and putting them together like a puzzle, or deep inside the Ark of the Covenant finding a Jivaro Indian shrunken head whose unstitched mouth sang Hebrew prayers.

Her only moments of respite were spent reading the *Black Insignia* books, but even here she was confronted with Daniel's story in every volume. In *The Diamonds of Madagascar*, it was children hiding at the bottom of a mine; in *The Bloodied Carpets of Lahore*, it was a little slave boy, the sole survivor of a massacre; in *Aunt Lucy's Cabin*, it was an orphaned Haitian girl torn between her two families; in *The Three Tigers of the Taiga*, it was an aging Mongol wandering the world to try to forget the wife and children he's lost.

She found more and more pleasure in reading the books. Although not fooled by the plot twists or the facile writing style, she let herself be carried away by the stories. But when she talked about them to Guillaume, she still didn't feel his childish enthusiasm. She pointed out the perennial triumphs of the good, generous white man, saving the dispossessed all over the world. That's not right, Guillaume protested, raising his voice and making his Adam's apple jut out from his neck, in Sanders's books the victims are never passive or defenseless, it's completely the opposite, they take the initiative, in fact

139

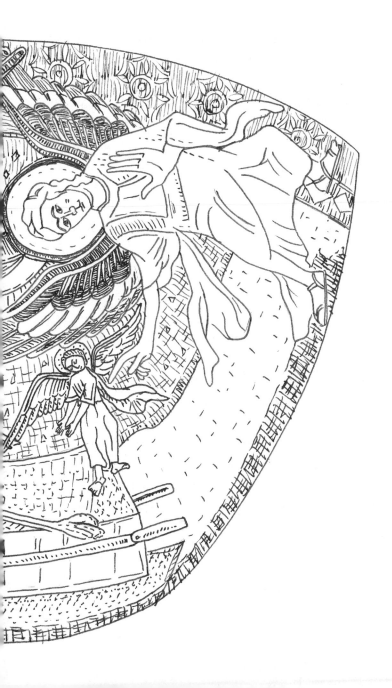

they often go to Peter's aid when he's in danger. Look at the women, especially younger women, they're bold and combative, like the young Roma girl in *The Road to Transylvania*, or the little servant girl in *The Soul Merchants of Bangkok*, or the teenage girl who unmasks the terrible headhunter in *The Black Cobra of Borneo*. He gave other examples, quoted passages, spoke as an expert. Running out of arguments, Hélène cited *The Warriors of Mururoa*, in which the three women in the crew play only auxiliary roles. The discussion became more heated, they found they were arguing about it, as if not talking about the same books at all.

THREE WEEKS AFTER SHE RETURNED FROM AMERICA, Hélène received a postcard. It was a view of Odessa, the courtyard of a dilapidated white house and its arched porch, with a caption translated into English, *Moldavanka, old Jewish quarter*, on the other side were just these few words, *Next year rue d'Odessa! Lots of love, Daniel*. So he was in the Ukraine, on the shores of the Black Sea, in the city that had given its name to the street where he grew up. She found the card reassuring, but slightly resented Daniel for disappearing without saying anything, at his age, like a runaway teenager. Anyway, the stamp was magnificent, a large ship with square sails, she put the postcard on her bookshelves to show Guillaume, who was also something of a philatelist.

He studied the stamp for a long time with the magnifying glass, the one Daniel had given Hélène. He was particularly interested in the postmark, ОДСÉА, УКРАЇНА, some of the letters weren't printed clearly and the ink was not the same throughout. He gave a sort of cry of triumph, the postmark was faked. Hélène took the magnifying glass now, perhaps Ukrainian postal workers franked the stamps by hand. Guillaume smiled, what are you talking about, Sanders did this. She couldn't see the point of going to so much trouble for the price of a stamp. No, no, come on, he put it into your mailbox himself, maybe he didn't even go to the Ukraine, he could have gone somewhere else, or just stayed in Paris, you can buy new postcards from all over the world and all sorts of stamps from those stalls along the banks of the Seine. Hélène immediately thought of the Vernaison market. She felt she'd been caught out, as if she'd cheated on Guillaume, as if Sanders, the globe-trotting writer, was not her great-uncle. But she hadn't actually invented anything, Daniel really had spent half his life traveling all over the world, she had proof of it, all those presents he'd brought back for her, like so many pebbles sown by Tom Thumb.

Guillaume, on the other hand, thought it was a wonderful stratagem, he punched his fist into his other hand

and started dancing around the room, looking as ridiculous as the mad sages who warn Tintin of the end of the world in *The Shooting Star*. He really was a big kid. As far as he was concerned, this fake postmark was just a clue in a treasure hunt. It reminded him of *The Call of Gibraltar*, which Hélène hadn't yet read, a book set in Tangiers in which Peter meets Ismaïl Seff, who makes false papers for emigrants. Guillaume loved the opening sentence, *Call me Ismaïl*. He leafed through the book to find the passage: *Ismaïl Seff's forgeries were perfect, but he sometimes took pleasure in smuggling in clues: for example he might add a feather to Hassan II's fez in an official stamp. He also falsified the postmarks on the postcards he sent to his friends. "Did you have a good trip?" they would then ask him, when Ismaïl had not actually set foot outside the old port.*

Hélène snatched the book from Guillaume, she didn't want to hear any more, she felt like having a fight, like throwing him out, more than anything else she felt like crying. Guillaume tried hard to persuade her that this trickery did nothing to detract from his admiration for Sanders, in fact it made his travels seem all the more incredible if they were invented, after all, Daniel Defoe had never left London and yet everyone still believed in the story of his Robinson Crusoe. Hélène wasn't listening. And there on that evening, in that low-ceilinged room, they didn't realize that this discovery, that meant such

diametrically different things to them both, heralded the unraveling of their relationship.

THE NEXT DAY HÉLÈNE WENT TO PICK UP JONAS from school to take him for a walk in the Luxembourg Gardens. In his pocket he had the little yellow taxi she'd brought back from New York for him. The apple trees were in blossom, Jonas opened his hand to show her a crumpled petal that he'd caught flying through the air, she said well done, but she wasn't really there with him. She was thinking about that postcard, wondering whether Daniel was really on the shores of the Black Sea, or actually in Little Odessa in New York, or perhaps rue d'Odessa in Paris, or somewhere else, anything was possible, she conjured a mental picture of him roving over a multicolored globe. And all those other times, had he really traveled or had he lied to them, to her and to all the others, for months, or even for years, perhaps all along? These questions rekindled the suspicions she'd had in the plane on the way home from New York, about Daniel and Suzanne, and the birth of Alain, her father. If Daniel was lying, if the postmarks couldn't be trusted now, nothing was sure anymore. Jonas had come over to her and was trundling the taxi up her leg, her arm, what are you thinking about, Hélène, look at my car, look at me, what are you thinking about?

THAT NIGHT GUILLAUME DIDN'T STAY WITH HER. She opened her bedside drawer and took out the postcards Daniel had sent her from Tierra del Fuego and Mauritania. She just wanted to check the postmarks, to reassure herself that her great-uncle wasn't an impostor. Studying it under the magnifying glass, she saw that the purple NOUAKCHOTT MAURITANIA postmark had the same imperfections as the Ukrainian one. Next she looked at the card from Tierra del Fuego, hoping that this one at least wouldn't let her down. How had she not noticed straightaway, even with the naked eye you could clearly see a J instead of an F in the postmark, in fact TIERRA DEL FUEGO had been turned into TIERRA DEL JUEGO, not land of fire but land of games.

21

L'Chaim

ON JUNE 11, PENTECOST SUNDAY, the Roche family celebrated Suzanne's seventieth birthday in Saint-Ferréol. They'd set up a long table in the open barn, and the young, such as Hélène, took on the job of serving the food. It was a very hot day, Aunt Paule was busying away indefatigably in the kitchen, you go and sit down Aunt Paule, I will, I will, a bit later. Glasses in hand, the guests started sitting on green or white plastic chairs, Suzanne had been seated at the head of the table. It was her sons, Alain and Thierry, who'd thought of having this birthday party, she'd been reticent at first, what's the point, without Maurice, but she'd let herself be persuaded, he would have liked to see her celebrating her birthday in Saint-Ferréol surrounded by the whole family.

Hélène's parents were there, of course, and Antoine, her brother, with his brand-new camcorder, Uncle Thierry, cousins from Saint-Amant-Roche-Savine, neighbors from Saint-Ferréol, some friends, at least thirty people, even Pascal, Aunt Paule's son, had made the journey for the occasion. Daniel hadn't come. He'd promised to, mind you, but he wasn't there. Since he'd come back from Odessa, or from God knows where, Hélène had only caught glimpses of him, he stayed at home working, he desperately needed to finish his latest book and deliver it to his editor. Late into the night she could see the light from behind his closed shutters, which he didn't open even during the day. In the mornings, Mrs. Almeida dragged the garbage cans across the courtyard as quietly as possible so as not to disturb Monsieur Roche, poor man, he was working *como um escravo*.

THE CHILDREN GOT DOWN FROM THE TABLE between courses and went to play the French game of bowls, *pétanque*, or to balance like tightrope walkers along the trunk of the great oak that had been uprooted in the December storm, now stripped of its branches and roots. Antoine filmed the guests, the feast, they'd been cooking for three days, he filmed the teenagers coming and going serving food, and the children scattered about the garden.

Before the dessert, Alain handed a rectangular parcel to Suzanne on behalf of everyone there, she slowly peeled off the wrapping paper with a mystified expression, even though she probably had her suspicions about what was inside, a gorgeous camera. Then they served the cake, which had been ordered from a patisserie in Ambert, it had a small rectangle of marzipan on top with the words *Happy Birthday Suzanne* and two candles, one shaped like a seven, the other like a zero. When everyone had a piece of cake, Thierry clinked his knife against his glass, and Hélène was immediately reminded of her grandfather who'd always done that to get everyone's attention around the table, he had the same voice, the same slightly solemn turn of phrase, in fact, as he neared fifty, Thierry was getting more and more like him. He talked about his father, and in his honor he broke into song with "Le Temps des cerises," a stirring piece associated with the courage and loss of life in the Paris Commune. Maurice had always sung it for his wife at celebratory meals, and now the older guests joined Thierry in the chorus, but the younger ones didn't know the words.

It was at this point that a taxi came to a halt on the road. Before even coming into the courtyard, when he was still on the far side of the gate, Daniel joined in with the others, singing as he drew closer, *And ever since then my heart has borne an open wo-o-ound*. The moment he saw Daniel step out of the taxi, Thierry had stopped singing.

By the end of the song, Daniel was coming through the gate and the children ran to meet him, Antoine, standing back slightly, filmed the scene. When the young had left him alone, Daniel kissed Suzanne. She was very touched,

I thought you wouldn't come, then he went around to each of them to say a personal hello, so, our little Parisian, late as usual, you've arrived in time for dessert, like the kids. He was quickly found a free chair and given a slice of cake, he mopped his brow and glanced around the table. Conversations gradually resumed where they'd broken off. He'd made a special effort to look smart, his hair neatly combed, clean shaven, a new shirt, the plastic loop from its price tag was still attached to the back of the collar. A few of the younger children came and tugged at his arms, asking him to join them at their end of the table to tell them stories, shhh, shhh, not right away.

Two women, a cousin and a friend, stood up and said a few words, complimenting Suzanne on how she was looking and expressing kind thoughts about Maurice, people sang and drank to each other's health, the men slumped against the backs of their chairs because of the heat, the women fanned themselves with paper plates.

Daniel stood up in turn, he'd never made a speech at a family gathering, it wasn't his style. Standing there with a full glass in his hand, which was shaking slightly, he dedicated a song to the Roche family, to my parents Angèle and Joseph, to my sisters, and to Maurice too, the Resistance fighter, my brother-in-law, my friend. Everyone knew that Maurice and Daniel had never got along, Hélène was amazed, this was like a reconciliation, like extending a handshake to Maurice, across the river. Perhaps it was also a revenge, Daniel would never have dared speak up like this in his brother-in-law's lifetime, until now he'd been happier staying to one side, being with the children, and putting on his usual performance, as if to prove right anyone who called him a clown, starting with Maurice. Out of the corner of her eye, Hélène watched Thierry, who was usually so calm, she thought he looked strained, he was refilling his glass, Suzanne was watching him, too, anxiously, she knew her son tried not to drink too much because he didn't hold it well. Alain, who was sitting on his mother's right, put his hand on hers every now and then, reassuringly.

Daniel raised his glass higher and said *L'chaim*, it means "to life" in Hebrew, and the guests responded, each in his or her own way, then he drank his glass down in one gulp and broke into a song by Georges Brassens, *Elle est à toi cette chanson, toi l'Auvergnat qui sans façon — This song is for you, my dear, you from the Auvergne who showed no fear*, and everyone who knew it joined in, there were more of them than there had been for "Le Temps des cerises."

Thierry didn't sing, he was looking at Daniel, he's no right to sing that, he hissed between his teeth, Hélène was close enough to hear him, despite the stirring voices. Suzanne heard him, too, but she pretended not to notice and carried on singing with the others.

TOWARD THE END OF THE AFTERNOON, people started to leave the table, the women shaking their skirts that had stuck to their thighs with sweat. The older guests went inside and sat in the cool of the house, while the young cleared the tables and the children sprayed each other with water bottles. Daniel went inside with Suzanne and the others, and they sat around the kitchen table, Aunt Paule, Hélène's parents, and a few cousins. Thierry had stayed outside, alone at one end of the long table, he'd lined up all the half-drunk bottles and was diligently emptying them one by one. When there was nothing left to drink, he headed unsteadily toward the house and, halfway there, he bent down and picked up a stone. Hélène was just coming out to get a chair, and he pretty much barged past her to get in, he smelled of wine, he positioned himself near the door, holding the stone behind his back. Everyone inside turned toward him, Hélène stayed on the doorstep, he said and now a speech for Daniel, my so-called uncle. For years now I've wanted to ask you why Alain always got the best presents, never me. Suzanne stood up, she was very pale, Thierry, I'm ashamed of you, and Alain put his hand around his mother's arm to stop her, let him speak, Mom. Thierry's blood was up, he was talking more and more loudly, the ten-speed bike, the stereo, and all that stuff, he was your favorite, he was always your favorite, you took his side even when he was wrong, can you explain why, what had I ever done to you. He was shouting now, unrecognizable, his face purple, you're not even my uncle, anyway, you're not part of this family, you're not from around here, do you get it, so get the hell out of here.

Daniel was opening his mouth to reply when Thierry suddenly stepped toward the table, Alain stood up to stop him but the younger man was taller and stronger than his older brother, he shoved him aside and, drunk though he was, he aimed well. Daniel just had time to duck to one side so the stone didn't hit him full in the face, it only grazed him. Everyone screamed, Suzanne more loudly than anyone else, Daniel brought his hand up to his temple and swayed in his chair but didn't fall, didn't cry out, it'll be fine, he kept saying, it'll be fine, he was ashen.

Two cousins had got to their feet to restrain Thierry, thinking he might throw himself at Daniel, but, as if horrified by what he'd done, he abruptly calmed down and stood there in the middle of the room with his arms hanging limply at his sides. One on either side of him, the cousins led him out into the courtyard, he went with them meekly. Daniel had quite a sizable wound, it was only skin-deep but it was bleeding a lot, and beneath it a large bruise was starting to appear. Suzanne was crying, Paule was talking about going to the emergency department, but Daniel refused, it wasn't worth it. Paule went to get the first aid kit, as a midwife, she was always the one who disinfected wounds and, to keep her sister busy, she asked her to help by handing her the compresses, even though her hands were shaking, you can manage. Suzanne apologized, I'm so sorry, she kept saying, as if it were her fault. Daniel patted her arm, don't you worry, Suzette, it'll be fine, he was smiling, very pale faced, dark rings around his eyes, do you remember, he said, I was sitting here, on this chair, the first time I met you, yes, I remember, the red pullover, he smiled, you see, I had a hard head then and I still have now.

The incident was over. It was incredible how highly strung Thierry was under his veneer of false calm, particularly since his divorce, and he couldn't hold his liquor, everyone knew that, but you couldn't watch over him like a child, he was nearly fifty. Luckily Daniel had good reflexes, he could have been badly injured, or worse, but thank the Lord it was nothing serious.

Hélène was still standing on the doorstep, and she could see Thierry sitting at the table outside, between the two cousins, his head in his hands, he looked as if he was crying, he'd go to sleep afterward, he always ended up falling asleep when he'd had too much to drink. Inside, Paule and Suzanne stood on either side of Daniel, still busy tending to him, Paule was winding a bandage around his head. Alain watched, sitting motionless, as pale as Daniel himself, then, pulling himself together, he tried to make a joke to ease the tension, that turban really suits you, yes, you're right, I'm going to let my beard grow, I'll look even more biblical. And it was true, the bandage gave him a dignified, venerable quality, somehow patriarchal. There in the half-light of that old house, the brother and his two sisters formed one of those scenes of sacred intimacy that you see in old paintings.

22

Marabout Sadi Alfa Maneh

IN HER HEART OF HEARTS, Hélène couldn't forgive Guillaume for noticing the faked postmarks and for admiring the hoax. She'd now read all twenty-three *Black Insignia* novels, she could have stuck a pin in a map of the world for each one of them, Senegal, Japan, Colombia, Polynesia, like planting a flag in a conquered country. She could no longer bear Guillaume's puerile enthusiasm, the way he talked about these adventures as if they belonged to him. *The Black Insignia* had brought them together, now it was coming between them. Of course he still knew the series better than Hélène, but there was one thing she knew that he didn't, why the cacique Umoro and the Carinaua were so angry with Peter, and she made a point of not telling him. She hadn't told him about the scene in Saint-Ferréol either, so as not to tarnish the Roche family image, but more particularly to avoid Guillaume feeling obligated to go and comfort Daniel.

They were slowly drifting apart. For several weeks they pretended not to notice, they carried on eating out at the Jade Lotus, then going back to her room together, sailing the China seas in their junk, but they didn't really believe it anymore. They still fell asleep huddled against each other like two spoons, but as the night wore on they moved apart without even realizing it, their elbows and knees knocking together as if the bed had suddenly become too small for two people, and they woke in the morning more like two knives.

HÉLÈNE HADN'T SEEN DANIEL IN PARIS since Suzanne's birthday. His shutters were permanently closed and, from the light that they allowed to filter out late into the night, she knew he was finishing his book. She was rather worried to see him cloistering himself in his apartment, his wound was only superficial but he should have gone to the doctor, or at least to the pharmacy, to have a new dressing. Perhaps he was avoiding going out so that he didn't have to answer any questions from neighbors and shopkeepers.

Hélène had handed in her dissertation on Germigny-des-Prés, but it was now time for her end-of-year exams, she worked at the institute all day and revised in her attic bedroom all evening. Still, she had called Daniel once to see how he was, he was absolutely fine, he wasn't in any pain, he was correcting his manuscript, I'm behind schedule, my editor's breathing down my neck, it's only a few hours' worth of work. She didn't pester him about dropping by to see him, he mustn't be disturbed at any cost.

AFTER THE EXAMS, Guillaume left for Central Asia where he was to spend the summer on a dig. As Hélène accompanied him to Roissy airport, she knew, as Guillaume did, that this departure would have no return for them, but they kissed as if they'd be seeing each other again soon. She watched his plane take off and waited until it disappeared into the sky. She hoped that the distance would make the breakup easier, but she was wrong. Years later she would still think of him, remembering his childishness that she found endearing and exasperating in equal measure. When she tipped over into adulthood, she would finally learn to recognize the child that lives on in each of us, like the heart of a tree beneath the bark. She would think that their relationship could have gone on longer, and without actually feeling regret, she would view it with a degree of nostalgia.

The evening Guillaume left, Mrs. Almeida could be heard talking noisily with a neighbor in the courtyard. She was no longer insisting on silence, so Daniel must have finished his twenty-fourth book. Hélène would have really liked him to lend her the manuscript, she was impatient to read Peter's latest adventures. She climbed up to her room with a sense of loss, almost pointlessness.

LATE IN THE EVENING she was leaning on the windowsill with a cigarette hanging out of her mouth, watching the last rays of sunlight over the rooftops, when she heard Daniel closing his window. She thought she could see a different light coming from behind the shutters, it was blinking like a bulb about to blow, or a dying flame, just for a few seconds, then everything went dark. She felt that after so many sleepless nights spent on his manuscript, Daniel must have gone to bed early, and she thought no more of it.

That night she dreamed she knocked at his door and the door swung open, she went in and found him asleep in his armchair, his beard had grown and he was wearing Grandpa Maurice's gray cap, she shook him and slapped him to wake him up, he waggled his head against the backrest as if saying no and didn't open his eyes, she lifted the cap and his temple started to bleed again. She woke up in the middle of the dream, and imagined all sorts of disasters, an infection in his wound, a blood clot, a brain injury. She thought back to what Thierry had done and wondered whether, hurt more by the insult than the blow itself, Daniel had committed suicide once he'd finished his book. The light she'd seen might have been a last sign before the darkness closed in. She felt guilty, she should have gone down to see him.

Usually, when a new day dawns, the previous night's anxieties look laughable, but it worked the other way that morning. Hélène could picture Daniel hanging in the corridor of his apartment, slumped on his desk covered in blood, drowned at the bottom of his bathtub, she knew it was her imagination but she couldn't help believing it. She rapped the lion's head knocker on his door for a long time, banged on the shutters in the courtyard, where she'd seen the flickering light, no one answered. She called him on her cell phone, and through the door she could hear the telephone ringing and the answering machine clicking on. This time she didn't ask the caretaker for help. She felt that if something had happened to Daniel, she was the only person who could help him, she had to find a way to get into his apartment but didn't yet want to call the emergency services to break down the door. Someone must have a spare key to his door, or even know where he was, one of his friends, the woman who sold candy, the man at the hardware store, Elie Frailich, Prosper perhaps. She remembered that when the marabout had given her his card, Daniel had told her not to forget his address, which might come in useful. She'd lost the card but, because there was so much promise in the name, she'd remembered 36 rue de la Goutte d'Or.

18e ARRt

RUE
DE LA
GOUTTE D'OR

LA GOUTTE D'OR, THE DROP OF GOLD, it was a name to fuel
dreams but a dreary street, even more disappointing than
rue d'Odessa. At number 36, a handsome but dilapidated
old building, there was an abandoned-looking travel goods
store. At the far end of the inner courtyard was a door
with flaking paintwork and a white plaque: PROFESSOR
MANEH, CONSULTATIONS, BY APPOINTMENT. Prosper
opened the door before she'd even knocked, he was wearing a light blue bubu, which made him look taller than
ever, come in, Hélène, I was expecting you. She was about
to tell him Daniel had disappeared but Prosper raised his
hands and said I know. He led her into a small square room
with one whole side screened off by a curtain, and gestured for her to sit on a divan. He himself sat in a wicker-
work armchair opposite her and stayed there in silence for
several minutes, with his eyes closed. Hélène found the
whole slow process unbearable, she felt he was going a bit
too far with his inspired marabout act, or was keeping her
waiting on purpose because he could see she was anxious.
He opened his eyes, she shouldn't worry, nothing had happened to Daniel, he just needed to recharge his batteries.
She was convinced Prosper knew exactly where Daniel
was, and she felt like calling him a charlatan. Recharge his
batteries, what did that mean, and what if her great-uncle
had come and hidden here with Prosper, maybe he was

actually at the far end of the room, she could hear someone breathing. She was staring pointedly at the curtain, so Prosper went over and drew it back, there were three beds in there, and a young man was asleep on one of them, he's my youngest son, he works nights.

Prosper sat back down in his wicker armchair and talked quietly, his long hands resting on his knees, I'm going to tell you an old story about my country, Casamance. Hélène shrugged, and he smiled, ah, the young, always impatient, it won't take long, and it might help you find your great-uncle. In the very last years of the slave trade, a young Diola woman is captured with the baby she's carrying on her back. The slave catchers stop for the night with their captives on the outskirts of a village, locals bring them flatbread to eat and earthenware jars full of water. When the slaves set off again, the young woman is carrying a jar where her baby had been. The overseers were put under a spell and didn't notice anything. One of the women from the village takes the baby home with her. She and her husband raise him as their own son. The boy grows up, has children and grandchildren and great-grandchildren, and sometimes he tells them the story of his two mothers, the one who abandoned him to save him, and the one who took him in. I'm one of those great-grandchildren. I sometimes think of my cousins in America, people I'll probably never meet.

He'd once confided this story to Daniel, who'd actually taken inspiration from it in one of his novels. Daniel also had two mothers, and, like Moses, had been abandoned by his parents in order to be saved, which was why, from time to time, he needed to stop being Daniel Roche and go back to being Daniel Ascher. That was most likely what he was doing now.

Prosper went behind the curtain and came back out holding a key. Hélène stood up, she didn't want to wait any longer, she asked whether Daniel had gone home or whether he was at rue d'Odessa. He's probably at home, said Prosper, not on rue d'Odessa anyway, he's never been back. When they'd first become friends, in the late '60s, the neighborhood had been handed over to bulldozers. The workshops that were left in Odessa Passage had been converted into makeshift theaters, but Daniel refused to go there, he wanted his memories to be left intact. When number 16 was about to be demolished, he'd asked Prosper to go and see whether he could salvage any possessions, some negatives from the Ascher studios perhaps, they could still be in a drawer. They'd already found photos on the sidewalk, among the debris, you wouldn't believe it, people sometimes throw out whole albums. At the time Daniel lived in the little room on the fifth floor of the building on rue Vavin, but not long after that he'd managed to buy the ground-floor apartment on credit.

In those days you could still find accommodation in that neighborhood without being as rich as Croesus. So I went to rue d'Odessa, I watched a digger ripping off the last strip of wall, everything was crushed under the tracked wheels, there was nothing left but rubble. When I told my friend all this, I saw how devastated he was, and I realized I was bringing an end to a long-held dream he'd never put into words, to go back and live on rue d'Odessa one day.

Prosper handed the key to Hélène, after dark, but not before, go to Daniel's apartment, go alone, close the door behind you, and look patiently, dig deep, like an archaeologist. Daniel hasn't disappeared, he hasn't crossed the Red Sea, you're not risking anything by opening his door, because he asked me to give you the key.

23

Return to Rue d'Odessa

HÉLÈNE WAITED TILL AFTER DARK to go down to Daniel's apartment. The door wasn't locked, and when she switched on the light in the hall she immediately spotted his parka hanging on a hook. There was a slight smell of burned wood, or rather of smoke gone cold. She closed the door behind her but stayed in the hallway, not daring to step farther into the apartment, fearing what she might find. Gradually, cautiously, she moved from room to room, switching on the lights as she went, in the living room, in the kitchen, where the dishes had been washed and that empty sink worried her, though she couldn't have said why. She gave a start as she walked into the bedroom, it looked as if a man was lying inert on the bed, but it was only the crumpled sheets that had assumed the shape of a body. She went back through every room, looking everywhere, in closets, behind curtains. Daniel was nowhere to be seen.

He must have a hiding place, though, a secret compartment, a cellar perhaps. She looked at the floor in the junk room, then the bathroom, she lifted carpets, the tiger skin, but found nothing. There were two identical brown suitcases in the bedroom, one standing by the door, the other lying on its side on the wooden floor, ready to be filled or emptied. She tried to pick it up, but it was impossible, it must be attached to the floor. When she opened it, it was empty, with a folded lap robe covering the bottom, this was hiding a trapdoor that she pulled up, and all at once light streamed out from down below. A voice drifted slowly up to her, intoning a song with no words.

Before slipping through the opening, she called a few more times, Daniel, Daniel Ascher, her voice louder and louder, no one replied. She climbed down the wooden staircase, stopping halfway down. She'd been expecting to find a cellar, but this was something else altogether, it was a second apartment, smaller and with lower ceilings than the one on the first floor, but more fully furnished, more inhabited, more alive. The walls were decorated in flesh-pink wallpaper and the floor completely covered with carpets in warm colors. The room in which she now stood was quite long, at one end was a dining area, furnished entirely in 1930s style, a square table with cut-off corners, four chairs, a sideboard, and at the other end was a living room with a divan, armchairs, a low bookcase, and an open phonograph with a record turning on it. She could hear it more clearly now despite the crackle of the stylus, what she'd thought was a voice was in fact a cello playing a slow old tune, sad as a kaddish. A display case hung on the wall, housing a collection of stones, exactly the same as hers, as if Daniel had bought them all in pairs, to give one to her and keep the other here. On top of the display case stood an old bronze menorah. The strangest thing was how many table lamps, floor lamps, and wall lights there were, they were all over the place, small golden lightbulbs lit up the room as if for a party. She didn't feel like an intruder, in fact she felt she was being greeted, welcomed, perhaps because of all these lights, which made you forget there were no windows, and the slightly heady amber smell that probably came from a lighted candle on the table.

There was a small kitchen in a recess and, behind a curtain under the stairs, there were deep shelves full of provisions of every sort, condensed milk, canned food, shampoo, crackers, and dozens of bags of sugar piled up like bricks, enough to survive a siege. Apart from these stores, nothing in the apartment was modern; it was a meticulous reconstruction of a prewar interior, even the stove and the cooking pots were from the period, as if time had stood still.

A door led to a second, smaller room with ocher-colored wallpaper, a bedroom with a single bed up against the wall, shelves filled with old books, and a desk with a writing case. A bathroom had been fitted into one corner, with a bathtub with lion's paw feet, and here, as with the rest of the place, all the lamps were lit. Hélène noticed some yellowed books next to a Jaz alarm clock with unmoving hands on the bedside table, and she suddenly realized that nothing in this underground home suggested travel, no suitcases ready for an imminent departure, no artifacts brought home from abroad, no maps, no guides. Just as the apartment upstairs was a stopping-off point, this one down here, its music, carpets, warm lighting, old wooden furniture, and heavy smell of amber, engendered a sort of languor, made you want to stay and never leave. Daniel was nowhere to be seen, but the phonograph playing and the candles implied he'd just been here and was still nearby.

On the far side of the bedroom, a door had been left ajar, Hélène opened it gently, she knew Daniel wouldn't be here. It was the smallest of the three rooms, its white walls and ceiling formed one continuous vault and were covered with dozens of black-and-white photos, portraits of men, women, children, married couples, families. Some bore the signature of Ascher Studios, others didn't, but they all had something in common, a recognizable armchair, a column, a carpet, and more particularly the same poses, the body at a slight angle, the head turned toward the camera. Hélène picked out Colette and Jim Peyrelevade on their wedding day, with little Daniel sitting cross-legged in the first row, and the photos of the Ascher family that she'd been shown in New York. They'd all been printed on very fine-grained, off-white matte paper and had been retouched in minute detail, making the oval of the subjects' faces a little too perfect. They were most likely portraits taken and retouched by Daniel's parents, in the Ascher Studios on rue d'Odessa. It felt to her as if all those faces almost took on a family likeness, that they reflected some of the photographer's kindliness in the moment when he captured their image.

A brown leather chair in the middle of the room beckoned to Hélène to sit down, its legs must have been sawn off, it was so low that she felt she was falling. Facing her was a framed photo, larger than the others. It was the last portrait of the Ascher family taken on Daniel's tenth birthday, the one she'd seen in a smaller version at Mala Seligman's apartment. The father looked like Daniel as she'd known him when she was a child, the mother with her slightly tired smile was wearing a dark dress and a brooch, her children had her eyes, almond eyes with long lashes, but the girl's face was too sharp and her expression too severe for her to be entirely pretty, her chestnut brown curls were held up by a barrette to one side, and she was wearing a polka-dot blouse. The little brother, with his buttoned-up jacket, was smiling so widely he had creases at the corners of his eyes, and a lock of curly hair lolled over his forehead. He was holding a book so small that his fingers almost completely

172

obscured its cover, but in this blowup of the picture you could make out the word WORLD. This framed photo stood on a set of shelves, on which there were also three lighted candles and a neat line of little pebbles.

Hélène gazed at those four faces for a long time, she was trying to find some anxiety in them, some suffering, a foreshadowing of calamity, but she saw nothing, they were serene, all smiles, brought together by their pose and by likenesses that the retouching process may have accentuated. The more she looked, the more interchangeable Isaac, Rywka, Hana, and Daniel became, and they blended with the reflection of her own face in the glass of the frame. She knew she'd come to the end, she couldn't go any farther, like when you reach the lowest stratum on a dig. She was no longer looking for Daniel; she'd found him. She was at 16 rue d'Odessa. The languorous feeling produced by the smell of amber was growing stronger and stronger, making her sleepy. Unable to fight it, Hélène let her head drop against the back of the chair and gave in to sleep.

SHE COULDN'T TELL HOW LONG SHE'D SLEPT, but the sound of a door being closed far away woke her. The chair was so low that she had to grasp onto the armrests to get up. A small gust of fresh air was circulating around the basement, dissipating the smell of amber and the lethargic

heaviness that went with it. The candle in the first room was no longer lit. A large picture above the divan attracted her attention, she hadn't noticed it earlier, perhaps because it was on the same side as the staircase. It was Soutine's *Girl with a Menorah*, the same as in her own bedroom, but this was a larger reproduction and it was in color. The young girl was in a pale yellow dress and she was in front of a dark blue wall, next to a bronze menorah. Her face and body were distorted, as if the painter had seen her through tears, but Hélène recognized Hana, with her chestnut curls pinned to one side, and her face that was too sharp to be entirely pretty. Her hands were clamped on her thighs and threw two scarlet shadows over the pale fabric of her dress, like two bloodstains. The sheen of her eyes was a blazing red, as if they were watching a huge destructive fire. Hélène could now see what made this portrait so unbearable. Soutine had painted everything that couldn't be seen in the photos, on those overly smooth, overly retouched images that harbored so many illusions and lies. He'd foreseen the torments to come, the blue of bruised bodies, the red of open wounds and firestorms.

Hélène climbed slowly back up the wooden staircase and out through the trapdoor in the brown suitcase. The other suitcase had gone. She didn't look around the apartment, she knew Daniel had left. There were four messages on the answering machine, including hers, but she didn't recognize her own voice. One was from Prosper, *Allah y hafdek, my brother, God keep you, I wish you fair winds*. The other two were from Daniel's editor, one left that same day, *Daniel, stop reworking your manuscript, let me read the thing, I'm sure it's great. You said it wasn't really an adventure story, it's too personal, but that's exactly why your loyal readers are going to love it. I sent you a courier but you didn't answer the door. I'm getting worried. Give me a sign of life, Daniel, I really need you to.*

He might have left his manuscript on the desk. If she found it, she'd be its first reader. But try as she might to find it, turning over the accumulated papers, she couldn't see it. All the files had been deleted from the computer's memory, images of the planets just drifted across the screen, indefinitely. She hoped that by searching through the notebooks and jotting pads scattered pell-mell around the place, she might exhume a rough draft, some fragments that would at least give her an idea of what this last book in the *Black Insignia* series would be like. She spent a long time studying the diagrams, drawings, and plans he'd sketched out, and opening screwed-up balls of paper. He'd clearly vacillated between a first- and third-person narrative, between Peter and Daniel. In the wastepaper basket she salvaged a list of titles with alterations and crossings-out: *Peter's Childhood, The Fall of the House of Ascher, The Travels of Daniel Ascher, The Last Book of Daniel.*

The smell of burning she'd noticed when she first came in was coming from the fireplace in the living room. The door of the wood burner had been left ajar. On top of some small charred logs lay a thick wad of paper that was completely burned up, she could make out only *For H* on the top sheet, the rest was illegible. She reached out to take it, but the moment she touched it, it dissolved between her fingers, dispersing into specks of ash. A gray and black dust so infinitely light that it hung in the air and settled on the wooden floor, this was all that was left of Daniel's last book. Hélène stayed kneeling in front of the fireplace for a while, too exhausted to stand up. If she'd come earlier, she could have saved the manuscript. She struggled to her feet and leaned against the mantelpiece. There on the marble, between the stuffed alligator and a Chinese terra-cotta soldier, she saw something new. It was an unassuming little book, no larger than a cigarette case. The title, *The Smallest Atlas in the World*, stood out against a background of brick-red continents and pale green oceans. On the first page she recognized the assertive handwriting from the postcard from Drancy. *On June 2, 1942, to my little* שלעמיל, *on his tenth birthday, to make you dream of traveling, Your sister, Annette.*

The beige parka was no longer on a hook in the hall. Hélène went back up to her room, taking *The Smallest Atlas in the World* with her, stowed deep in her pocket.

IN HER BEDROOM she leafed through the little book under the glare of her lamp. Some pages had annotations in black pencil, in extraordinarily small handwriting, and she managed to read them using the old horn-handled magnifying glass.

On the first planisphere, the pale blue background of seas and oceans was filled with writing, *I have told many stories, never my own, I have made up twenty-three adventures, but when I tried to write the last one, the real one, about someone who was left behind, who is left here still, who is left without words, who is left to live his life after all the others have gone, I could not do it, my memory betrayed me, I betrayed their memory, I abandoned the task, afraid I would not be worthy of it, can anyone be worthy of the dead, I took my pages and I burned them, perhaps one day someone will be able to write this book for me,*

On the map of *Western USSR*, a tiny ribbon of text had its source in the Black Sea, just where the name *Odessa* was printed, and it went like this, *Odessa was the name of an eastern princess who had magnificent baths built in Paris, embellished with emeralds and turquoise, my father takes me there on Friday evenings,* then the words climbed northward, skirting around Kiev, Minsk, and Smolensk, crossing Russia and losing themselves on the icy plains toward Arkhangelsk on the banks of the White Sea,

Germany punched great fists into the flesh pink of Poland; Kamieńsk, which was too small to feature, had been added by hand to the south of Łódź, the close-knit lines of numerous railways left little room for the words to continue with their journey, *in his darkroom my father counts the seconds in Polish, jeden, dwa, trzy, cztery, because Polish is exactly the right length of time, he and my mother and sister tell each other secrets in Yiddish, they think I'm a schmuck,*

setting off from Jerusalem, the sentences ventured toward the East and Arabia, racing over the arid sands of Hedjaz and Nedjed, *every year when we say the blessings for Yom Kippur, we huddle under my father's prayer shawl as if it were a tent, and the courtyard at the synagogue is like a small-scale desert encampment,*

under the table *Races and religions*, beneath the columns *Catholics, Protestants, Jews, Confucians*, a single line, *one day, on the door to my baths, No entry for Jews, the end of the world,*

the table of *Principal means of transport, railroads, commercial fleets*, left just enough room for words to weave between the names and numbers, *Sister Annette, Sister Annette, did you not see any of this coming, my sister who feels farther from me than Paule or Suzanne, I never shared her room, never knew anything about her dreams, Hana, seven years older, seven times better behaved, follow her example, Daniel, you never listen, jealous of her for going with her mother, jealous of her death even,*

in order to see France you had to tilt the atlas, it was cut horizontally by the crease in the middle of the page, the sentences snaked along the coastline, tracing out an increasingly sinuous maze over the seas, *the woman traveling with me is reading the paper but not turning the pages, I don't know her real name, we take several trains, walk a long way in the dark, depending on the time of day my terror swells or vanishes, forgotten, on a moonless night I cross a river, probably the Cher, in a boat steered by a wordless ferryman with silent oars, it is wide as an ocean, on the far bank another woman, dressed in black, is waiting for me, Daniel Ascher has become Daniel Roche,* the two pages overlapped slightly, hiding a whole strip of land, right where Clermont-Ferrand and Ambert should have been, *the Livradois region is invisible, it's the safest place in the world, they'll never find me here,*

the table for the world's largest islands and highest peaks was loaded with lines of writing cramped together in the margins, *when the bus stops a woman takes my suitcase and pulls me under her umbrella, inside the house an old lady talks as if I were a baby, he's all wet, he needs changing, give him a bowl of milk, it's Grandma Guyon, and it's Angèle,* and farther on, *Joseph's palms are as hard as pebbles, he sometimes puts his hand on my head, he's always wanted a son to take over the farm handed down from his father and his grandfather, could I be that son,*

along the jagged coast of Scandinavia, on the sinuous image of the Baltic Sea, the writing was more and more cramped, barely legible, *in Saint-Ferréol in winter boys play games peeing in the snow, I run over with my hand on my fly and stop myself at the last minute, that's a stupid game, no one here has seen me naked, not even Angèle, I wash very quickly, especially in winter, my filth keeps me warm,*

other sentences zigzagged between the archipelagos of Oceania, *to read the names of the Micronesian archipelagos in my little atlas I gently take Grandma Guyon's glasses when she's dozed off in her armchair, Solomon Islands, Erromango, Vanua Levu, I sail between the atolls for a few minutes, here are your glasses, Grandma, you went to sleep, no, my little goose, I wasn't asleep, I was resting, even when she snores, Grandma Guyon's never asleep,* on the lists of average temperatures, from Algiers to Spitzberg, of the most populous states, and the most widely spoken languages, lists that leave few spaces, the words battled to pick out a halting, angular route, *I can't remember when I stopped hoping they would come back, for a long time I dream my parents come home and I don't recognize them, or I refuse to go with them, I can see the reproach in their eyes because I've been happy without them, I see my parents, never my sister,*

on the *Time zones* page, a white world with red stripes, the contorted penciled lines covered the expanse of the Antarctic Ocean and converged toward the South Pole, growing increasingly hurried and untidy, making them unreliable to read, *being the wanderer, the man with no shadow, not knowing the place, not knowing the date, no yahrzeit, no kaddish, not knowing how they died, and imagining all sorts of possible deaths, endlessly, did they think they were taking a shower, were they still clutching a piece of soap in their spasming hands, imagining the moment when they realized, hoping it was as late on as possible, just in time to recite the Shema Yisrael and to cover their heads, but how do you cover your head when you're naked,*

on the vast plains of North America, the words were back in their stride, *I once read a piece about Indians who take the bones of their dead everywhere with them, rolled up in a blanket, I am an Indian,* and on the blue of the Atlantic, along the East Coast, *my Aunt Mala made me promise to come back and see her before she died, she wanted to give me something, she's so old, she must be tired after all these years spent living instead of her sister, when I go back to New York she can finally let herself die,*

in South America, the sentences cut across the Amazon tributaries, Purus, Madeira, Tapajos, Xingu, venturing out, *in order to tell the story of this Peter Schlemiel I need to find a pseudonym, Ascher means happy in Hebrew, a heavy name to bear, Ash-err, full of firestorms and aimless wandering, how to disguise these ominous, onerous meanings, hide them behind two letters, H. R., which in French would be pronounced Ascher, and then Sanders, which conjures sand as well as cinders, but I've also kept the name of the Roche family who saved my life, roch means head in Hebrew, with these two names I am flesh, I am in my head and I am cinders, all at the same time,*

at the foot of the index page, where there was a blank space, verses that were an eerie distortion of the Book of Daniel had been carefully written out,

And so Daniel and his friends were sought out to be killed, All those whose names were inscribed in the Book,

They were bound and thrown into the blazing furnace,
The wind bore them away and left no trace,
Then Daniel was taken from the furnace and found to be
unharmed,

and on the blank double-page spread at the end of the tiny book, in tightly spaced lines, *for the first time in all these years, I've dreamed of you at last, Hana, you were asleep on the divan in the living room like when I used to wake you as a practical joke on Sunday mornings and you'd call me a little idiot, but you didn't scold me this time, you got up and you looked just as you did when I last saw you, I was happy, wonderfully happy, I said so you're alive and there I was thinking, what were you thinking, little idiot, I was in the room upstairs, you were mussing my hair, where did you get all these white hairs, little schlemiel, you're only ten, so I whispered, they're the hairs of a grandfather, a long time ago, my soul sister secretly gave me a son, and he had two children of his own, his daughter looks like you, she has your eyes, Hana, you can sleep easy, one day our descendants will be as plentiful as the stars in the sky.*

Epilogue

JULY 16, 2012

SHE'D NEVER NOTICED THIS VIDEOTAPE sitting among the others, labeled only with a date, June 11, 2000. She slips it into the video player and the twelve-year-old images appear on the screen, intact. Her father laughing, his hairline barely receding, the little cousins walking along the fallen tree trunk, their arms out for balance, her mother there, too, Aunt Paule in the kitchen, Suzanne, everyone else, and herself, tray in hand, sticking her tongue out to the camera, they're all so young. People raising their glasses, women fanning themselves, someone calling, Antoine, film this, there's a close-up of the cake. They sing "Le Temps des cerises," the camera pans around the table, moves over toward the gate, frames Daniel who's also singing, *will never ease my pain.*

Then the camera goes around the back of the house and down to the bottom of the garden, you can just make out two figures, Daniel in a pale blue shirt and Suzanne in a flowery dress, in the shade of the apple tree, it's before the row with Thierry, Daniel isn't bandaged. The shot

185

zooms in, bringing them closer but the image is shaky, you can't see their features, they're too far away to hear what they're saying, Daniel puts his hand on Suzanne's shoulder, she shakes her head, she touches his cheek, from the way her shoulders move it looks as if she's crying, he moves closer to her, she opens her arms, and the film stops.

Hélène plays the scene again, tries to make out the faces, to work out whether Suzanne was already crying before Daniel joined her, but perhaps there's something else that fascinates her, something she should never have seen. She watches it one more time, and then another, those wobbly images, those silent figures in the shade of the orchard, the movement of two bodies coming together, like an interrupted dance step, left in suspense.

SHE SWITCHES OFF THE VIDEO and sits back into her chair, the only armchair in the living room. Nothing has changed for twelve years, the tiger is losing his last hairs, the alligator is losing his sheen on the mantelpiece, the Jivaro with stitched lips is gently gathering dust, and everywhere in Daniel's apartment, as there always were, there are piles of books, maps, and newspapers. The day he returns from his travels, if he ever returns, he'll find his shambles just as he left it.

THE SUMMER SHE TURNED SEVENTY, Suzanne took a plane for the first time, to listen to the whale songs in the Gulf of Saint Lawrence. She sent Hélène a postcard with the postscript *The postmark is the REAL thing*. She's traveled a lot since then, she's been to New York, Verona, Odessa, Jerusalem, she's come home with beautiful photos, and she's never forgotten, on every trip, to send a postcard. Hélène knows Suzanne isn't telling her everything, she knows who it is she's meeting in each destination, but she doesn't resent her for keeping this last secret.

And in those twelve years she too has traveled to distant countries, worked on digs, exhumed mountains of skeletal remains, and more particularly reassembled tens of thousands of Byzantine mosaic tiles, her specialty. She's kept the key to Daniel's apartment, and she sometimes comes and spends a few hours here, when everyone thinks she's gone off on some job. She goes down to the basement and sits in the very low armchair in the vaulted room with all the photos, sometimes she even sleeps.

But today, after watching the video, she stays in the living room. Motes of dust dance in the lamplight. They must still include minute particles of the burned manuscript. She was wrong to think it had gone. It's still here, hanging in the air, it would take only one puff of breath to make it spiral and glitter in the light.

Hélène sits down at the desk. She sharpens a pencil in the sharpener with a crank handle, until it comes to a perfect point, like the tip of a harpoon. She opens a blank notebook, rests her elbow amid the piles of books, cards, and notebooks, and the pencil in her hands sails over the white ocean of paper, starting to tell the story of Daniel Ascher.

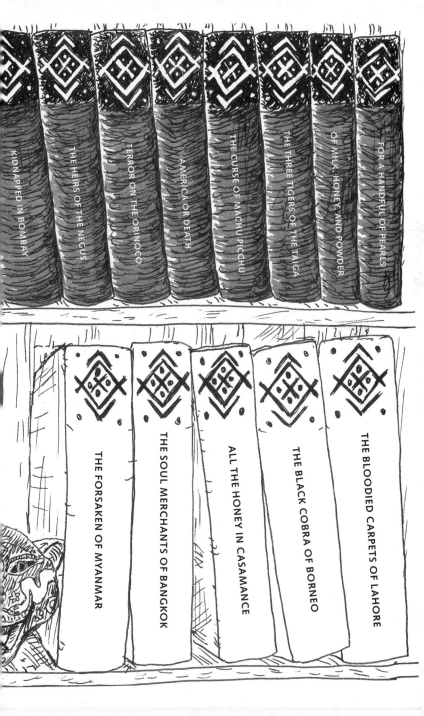

ALREADY PUBLISHED IN THE COLLECTION
"THE BLACK INSIGNIA"

The Ferrymen of the Amazon
The Road to Transylvania
The Warriors of Mururoa
Aunt Lucy's Cabin
The Diamonds of Madagascar
Kidnapped in Bombay
The Heirs of the Negus
Terror on the Orinoco
America or Death
The Curse of Machu Picchu
The Three Tigers of the Taiga
Of Milk, Honey, and Powder
For a Handful of Pearls
The Bloodied Carpets of Lahore
The Black Cobra of Borneo
All the Honey in Casamance
The Soul Merchants of Bangkok
The Forsaken of Myanmar
The Scarab of Henuttaneb
The Call of Gibraltar
Meet Me in Soweto
The Clay Army of Xi'an
Theft in the Fugitives' Garden

DÉBORAH LÉVY-BERTHERAT lives in Paris, where she teaches comparative literature at the École Normale Supérieure. She has translated Lermontov's *A Hero of Our Time* and Gogol's *Petersburg Tales* into French. *The Travels of Daniel Ascher* is her first novel.

ADRIANA HUNTER studied French and Drama at the University of London. She has translated more than fifty books including *Eléctrico W* by Hervé Le Tellier, winner of the French-American Foundation's 2013 Translation Prize in Fiction. She won the 2011 Scott Moncrieff Prize and has been short-listed twice for the Florence Gould Foundation Translation Prize. She lives in Norfolk, England.